Other Books in the Growing Faithgirlz!™ Library

Fiction

From Sadie's Sketchbook

Shades of Truth (Book One)

Flickering Hope (Book Two)

Sophie's World Series

Sophie's World

Sophie's Secret

Sophie Under Pressure

Sophie Steps Up

Sophie's First Dance

Sophie's Stormy Summer

Sophie's Friendship Fiasco

Sophie and the New Girl

Sophie Flakes Out

Sophie Loves Jimmy

Sophie's Drama

Sophie Gets Real

The Girls of Harbor View

Girl Power

Rescue Chelsea

Raising Faith

Secret Admirer

Check out www.faithgirlz.com

From Sadie's Sketchbook

Flickering Hope

Book Two

Naomi Kinsman

ZONDERVAN.com/
AUTHORTRACKER
follow your favorite authors

We want to hear from you. Please send your comments about this book to us in care of zreview@zondervan.com. Thank you.

ZONDERKIDZ

Flickering Hope
Copyright © 2011 by Naomi Kinsman Downing

This title is also available as a Zondervan ebook.
Visit www.zondervan.com/ebooks

Requests for information should be addressed to:

Zonderkidz, Grand Rapids, Michigan 49530

ISBN 978-0310-72664-7

Editor: Kim Childress
Cover design: Cindy Davis
Interior design and composition: Greg Johnson/Textbook Perfect

Printed in the United States of America

12 13 14 15 /DCI/ 20 19 18 17 16 15 14 13 12 11 10 9 8 7 6 5 4 3 2

For my parents, who taught me to believe in
Christmas miracles, big and small.

Chapter 1

Pea-Soup Gravy

Pots and pans and spilled spices filled the research cabin's tiny kitchen. Pumpkin pies cooled on top of the washing machine. Turkey, bread, and mashed potatoes warmed in the oven. I brushed flour off Ruth's nose and grinned at Andrew. He smiled his crooked half-smile and waved olive-topped fingers.

"No fair. We're not done cooking!" I said.

"Olives are an appetizer, Sadie." He brought the tray over.

Ruth and I slipped olives onto our fingers, and I felt six years old instead of twelve. In the good way, the way you can only feel when you're with friends you trust, and you're all in it together. One by one, we popped olives into our mouths until our cheeks bulged. We laughed as we watched each other chew. Happiness fizzed through me, sweet and bubbly, like the sparkling apple cider chilling outside in the snow.

Andrew and I had spent almost all of November begging his mom, Helen, to host Thanksgiving dinner.

Helen had smoothed back the black wispy hairs that never failed to escape from her signature French braid. "We don't have the space! It's a research cabin, not a house."

Still, she and Andrew lived here. One main room filled the cabin's first floor, serving as kitchen, living room, and dining room, with Helen's paper-strewn office in the back. Andrew and Helen's rooms, the bathroom, and one guest room made up the second floor. The mudroom overflowed with boots, snowshoes, poles, and winter gear for trekking out into the woods and monitoring dens. Photographs of Helen's research subjects, the now-hibernating bears, lined the log walls. Andrew and I had known Thanksgiving at the cabin would be messy and crowded and perfect. We had promised to help cook and do all the clean up, and even to snowshoe the four miles out and back to check on Patch's den after dessert so Helen could have a true day off.

When my family moved to Michigan three months ago for the start of my seventh grade, I had pictured moments like this one—moments full of new friends and fun. You just can't have a stuffy Thanksgiving dinner in a log cabin.

"Aha!" From the other side of the washing machine, Dad pulled his head out of the spice cabinet and did a victory dance, holding up a box of food coloring. Flour billowed off his sandy-blonde hair. Somehow, he missed the cooking lesson in which they tell you not to run your fingers through your hair.

"We'll dye the gravy!" he announced.

Mom and Helen looked up from their conversation. Mom hid her smile behind a mug of tea. The lines often so tight around her eyes were relaxed today, and color filled her cheeks.

Mom had refused to participate in gravy-making. She baked the pies and mashed the potatoes but drew the line on gravy, which never came out right for her anyway. Helen had poured turkey juice into the pot and added spices and cornstarch. Still, the gravy was too soupy. Dad stepped in, but his excessive use of flour turned the gravy white.

As he passed me the food coloring, Dad said, "Come on, Sadie, put those art lessons to use. No one wants to eat ghostly gravy."

Ruth and I squeezed red and yellow and blue and green drops into the pot and stirred. Higgins jumped up, muddying the cupboard door with his too big puppy paws.

I pushed Higgins away. "Down, Higgy!"

Of course he jumped back up, his brown ears flopping and his rope-like tail thwapping our legs. Dad and Andrew supervised the color-mixing over our shoulders. When I squeezed the final yellow drop into the gravy and all the coloring was used up, we stepped back.

Andrew nodded, a very serious look on his face. "Much better."

We dissolved into laughter. The gravy was pea-soup green.

As Andrew set the gravy boat out on the counter, Ruth's family plowed up the snowy driveway in their SUV. Her parents stomped snow off their boots in the entryway and untangled themselves from coats and hats and mittens, while her twin brother and sister circled them in a left-over game of tag.

"Happy Thanksgiving!" Ruth's dad said. "We had twenty people at our last service this afternoon. Everyone came to church early so they could hurry home to feast."

"You're just in time." Helen hugged Ruth's parents and the twins, who stood as still as could be expected. "Make yourselves at home."

We arranged plates and silverware and hot platters of food on the countertop, buffet style.

"Rick, will you say a blessing?" Helen asked Ruth's dad. "As our resident preacher?"

I was surprised. Helen never went to church, and I didn't think she prayed over meals. But maybe Thanksgiving was different. After an awkward moment of people first closing their eyes, then bowing their heads, then looking around and closing their eyes again, the rustling settled.

"God, thank you for the joy of an afternoon with family and friends. Thank you for this abundance of food and for the many blessings you've brought this year—health and safety and peace. Help us be a blessing to one another. Amen."

As we opened our eyes, I watched Mom turn to kiss Dad on the cheek. Could Mom finally become healthy? *Please let it be possible.*

I piled my plate with mashed potatoes and jello salad and took the smallest possible piece of turkey, which I'd pass off to Higgins when no one was looking.

Andrew, Ruth, and I sat on the couch. The twins sat at the table, because the table only seated four, the extra adults perched around the living room and kitchen with their plates.

I shoved my mashed potatoes to the far side of my plate so the melting jello wouldn't contaminate them.

"So how's the food-fight queen? Is Frankie back yet?" Andrew kept his voice low.

None of us wanted to launch the adults onto the topic of hunters, or specifically, Frankie's hunter-dad Jim who had it in for Patch.

Ruth swirled gravy into her mashed potatoes, turning the entire lump green. "It's been two weeks, so maybe she's not coming back."

"I'm worried," I said. "It doesn't seem like her friends know where she went."

"Come on, Sadie. She calls you Zitzie. You can't really miss her," Ruth said.

I pushed Higgins away from Ruth's plate. "Frankie only called me Zitzie when I had all those mosquito bites."

"If something was truly wrong, we'd have heard," Andrew said.

We dug into our food, relieved when the twins finished eating and chased Higgins around the living room, so we no longer had to defend our plates from dog-slobber.

"Dessert now or after the hike?" Andrew asked.

Ruth grabbed our plates. "Now. And maybe afterwards, too."

I helped load the dishwasher while Andrew glopped mounds of whipped cream onto each piece of pie. Mom had made her famous praline crust. We settled back onto the couch, and I took a slow bite, letting the brown sugar and butter melt on my tongue.

"That's it. Next year, we're doing Thanksgiving exactly like this." Ruth stopped, her fork halfway to her mouth. "You'll be here next year, right Sadie?"

I shrugged. "I don't know how long the Department of Natural Resources will need Dad."

"At least through hunting season next fall," Andrew said. "Things heat up when the bears come out of hibernation. The DNR will need him to mediate then."

I nodded, but even the familiar, comforting taste of Mom's pumpkin pie couldn't take away the uneasiness that slithered into my stomach. This was home now. I didn't want to pick up and start again, especially now that I understood how hard starting over could be.

I ate my last bite of pie slowly, savoring it, and then said, "Let's go hike. Before my stomach explodes."

"Stick to the path," Helen called from the table. "And make sure you cover up your tracks close to the den, Andrew. The whole point is keeping Patch safe."

Andrew rolled his eyes. "Yes, I know, Mom."

But Andrew worried about Patch just as much as his mom did, especially now, after he and I had overheard Frankie's dad, Jim, threaten to find Patch in her den. Now, more than ever, Patch needed our help.

Chapter 2

Snow Quiet

Upstairs in the guest room, Ruth and I yanked and pulled and zipped ourselves into our gear. Ruth and Andrew always expected me to dress wrong for the weather, being from California. But my family had skied in Tahoe almost every year, so I knew how to dress for cold.

I caught our reflection in the mirror—Ruth, tiny, swallowed up in her red ski coat and pants, her black hair entirely hidden under her striped red hat, and me, looking like the Jolly Green Giant in my lime green coat and dark green pants. I was a normal height for my age, but next to Ruth, I looked enormous. As usual, curly hair escaped my braids in every direction. We'd struck a deal about this, my hair and I. Each morning, wet and well-behaved, my hair allowed itself to be woven into braids, which artfully decomposed through the day into a mess that, at least, didn't resemble bed-head.

I pulled on the purple stocking cap topped with a fuzz ball that Pippa, my best friend from California, had sent me as a first-snow present. Ruth and I waddled out into the hall. Andrew came out of his room and slammed the door behind him.

"What? Is your room a *total* mess again?"

Andrew thought a few misplaced papers was a catastrophe.

"No." Andrew blocked my way.

I dodged past and pretended to turn the doorknob. "You sure?"

He yanked my hand away. "Knock it off."

"What if we already peeked in?" I grinned at him. "When we first came upstairs."

Andrew frowned, his eyebrows scrunching together. "Did you?"

"Maybe."

"No really, Sadie, did you?"

His mouth pressed into a tight line and real anger flashed in his eyes. Normally teasing was no big deal for Andrew.

I raised my hands in mock surrender. "Kidding, Andrew. No big deal."

He didn't smile. When I stepped back, he walked word-lessly away. Ruth raised an eyebrow at me. I shrugged, laced my arm through hers, and we followed Andrew downstairs.

We sat on the edge of the deck to strap on our enormous snowshoes. I had never worn snowshoes before, but I wasn't about to tell that to Ruth, or Andrew, especially after his freak-out upstairs.

I stood, took one step, and tumbled into a snowdrift. Ruth snorted and burst into giggles.

"Last one to the trees has to scrub the turkey pan!" Andrew called, tramping out into the knee-deep snow as though walking on a perfectly groomed trail.

I brushed white powder off my gloves and shook it out of my hair. "Cheater!"

When I took another step, I almost fell again. Ruth caught me on the way down and yanked me upright.

"You have to bend your knees," Ruth said.

I swung one foot up and over the snow and transferred my weight, finally getting the swing-stomp by the time we reached the trees.

Andrew's red hat bobbled up and down in the distance. Ruth and I moved in rhythm, avoiding snow that fell off the pine needles above in icy glops.

I wrapped my scarf tight so the wetness couldn't slip down my back. "What was that all about? Do you think Andrew's hiding something? A picture of a girl he likes or ...?"

Ruth raised an eyebrow at me. "No way, Sadie."

I didn't want Andrew to have a picture of another girl in his room. And I didn't want to consider why Andrew's secret was so important to me.

I tried to decide which would feel better—falling face-first into the snowbank to cool down my burning cheeks, or screaming as loud as I could—when suddenly Ruth held out her arm, blocking my path. "Look."

We stepped out of the trees into a meadow. Aside from Andrew's tracks, the unmarked snow stretched to the distant trees from our right to left. We stood listening to the snow quiet.

"Do you ever feel like you could just turn a corner and step into Narnia?" Ruth asked. "Like ... anything is possible?"

Ruth looked out at the snow, her face lit up, almost glowing. Was anything possible? Could Andrew ... Even the first few words of that thought made me want to run. Andrew was my friend, and hoping for more would ruin everything. I took a deep breath and wiggled around so thoughts of Andrew would disappear from my mind. He wasn't the only impossibility in my life.

Mom. Every disease I knew of, even the bad ones like cancer, had treatments. But somehow Mom had been cursed with a disease with no treatment. Chronic Fatigue Syndrome, a disease doctors couldn't understand, couldn't predict. Instead of fixing her, they suggested experiments. Try vitamins. Try rest. Lower your stress level. Exercise. Don't exercise. Still, exhaustion crept up on Mom, pounced on her when we least expected it, ruined birthdays, holidays, vacations. Good days when Mom was finally present, free from the monster inside her, only reminded me of what I missed the rest of the time. And good days could end any second.

Ruth stood still, her long lashes dusted with snowflakes. Sometimes I wanted to tell Ruth everything, about Mom, about my questions, about me. I wanted to turn myself inside out and show her and see if I was okay. Pippa knew many of my secrets, not because I had chosen to share them, but because she had experienced most of them right along with me. Ruth was different. She only knew the parts of me I chose to share.

I stood right on the edge, wondering if I should step over.

Ruth grabbed my elbow, interrupting my thoughts. "We've got to catch Andrew. Up there, no one has made a single track. Think of how amazing it must look."

She took off faster than I imagined snowshoes could ever go. I stumbled through the snow after her, fell on my knees, and pulled myself back up, laughing the whole time. Steam billowed out of the neck of my coat. I took it off and tied it around my waist, still walk-running to keep up with Ruth.

We plunged back into the trees, following Andrew's tracks. Finally, we saw his red hat.

"Andrew, wait up!" Ruth called.

When we caught up with Andrew, he led us off to our right. "The den is up this hill. Walk quietly now and muss your tracks."

We zigzagged between trees to disguise our path. About a hundred feet away from the hillside where Patch had dug out her den under a rock, we stopped. I could barely see the exposed part of her black, furry back, almost entirely covered with snow. She and her yearlings had filled most of the gap with dirt and leaves after they had climbed into their den, a process which Andrew and I, amazingly, watched over a month ago. A small section of the gap was still open for air circulation. For a long moment, we watched snowflakes fall on Patch's black fur, and then we backed away from the den.

A safe distance away, Andrew said, "If only we knew the bears will be safe all winter."

I nodded, not able to put my similar wish into words that expressed just how much I hoped for Patch's safety. I slowed my pace, listening to snow melting and dripping off the pine needles. Then, I stopped, hearing a noise behind me. Rustling in the bushes. I listened.

Nothing happened.

I walked toward the bushes and crouched down to peer into the snow-covered pines. Two huge green eyes stared back at me.

At first, I couldn't breathe. The small girl, who couldn't be much older than Ruth's brother and sister, held her finger to her lips. "Don't let them see me."

Words caught in my throat. What could I say to this dirt-streaked little girl? What was she doing out here, alone in the forest, in the vicinity of Patch's den?

As I turned to check if Ruth and Andrew had seen, the girl gripped my arm with freezing-cold fingers, so cold I could feel the chill through my thermal shirt. "Promise you won't tell anyone about us living out here."

My mind spun. This little girl lived out here? With who? Why? How did they keep warm? When I didn't speak, the girl squeezed tighter, her fingers surprisingly strong.

"Promise, or I'll tell my dad the bears are near here."

Her narrowed eyes and fierce grip told me this wasn't an empty threat. Without meaning to, we had led her straight to Patch's den. The girl shook my arm again, demanding a response.

The words slipped out of my mouth before I could stop them. "I promise."

The girl took off through the snow, as fast as she could in her worn boots. Long, tangled brown hair swung across her back.

"Hey!" Andrew called out behind me.

The girl turned back, saw Andrew and Ruth, and glared at me, a warning clear in her eyes. But what warning? Haze filled my mind, as though I'd woken from a deep sleep. Broken bits of our conversation ricocheted off one another, making less sense the more I thought about them.

"What did she say to you?" Andrew put his hand on my shoulder. "Sadie?"

I realized I was cradling my arm, staring down at the muddy stains the girl's fingers had left behind. The girl had almost disappeared into the trees.

"We have to follow her," I said.

Our snowshoes made it almost impossible to run, but we stumbled forward as fast as we could, managing to keep the girl in sight, though just barely. When we stepped through the thick bushes into a clearing, Andrew held out his hand to stop us. A wooden shack slumped in the distance. Smoke rose from a metal pipe stuck at an angle in the roof.

We leapt behind the bushes as the shack door swung open, and a man in a flannel shirt, orange hunting vest, and knee-high boots stepped out into the snow. Behind him, a woman stood, concern clear on her face. She cradled a baby against her shoulder.

"Where've you been?" the man asked. "You left for the outhouse fifteen minutes ago."

The baby whimpered, and the woman stepped back as the man laid his arm protectively across the little girl's shoulders and led her inside. He closed the door, rattling the shotgun that leaned up against the cabin steps.

Chapter 3

Shut Out

"That's Old Man Mueller's shack," Andrew whispered. "Well, it's the shack he squats in during the summer. But I've never seen those people before. I'm sure Old Man Mueller doesn't have family. The shack isn't really his, but no one stops him from staying there. The company that owns this land gave up on ever selling it and basically ignores the old man."

Ruth bit her lip. "A baby shouldn't be out in the forest like this. She'll freeze."

Andrew brushed snowflakes off his jacket. "Let's head out. We're too exposed here."

As we circled around toward the research cabin, I thought about the girl, my promise, and Patch. Patch had been in danger even before she went into hibernation. After she had nuzzled Jim Paulson's hand last September, he decided she was dangerous. At the community meeting people from the area defended the bears, but Jim wouldn't listen. To him, Patch was a problem only a gun could fix.

Andrew and I had thought until a few weeks ago that hibernation would protect Patch. We were sitting in our favorite pair of cushy chairs behind the bookshelves at Black Bear Java. Jim and Mack had come in, talking loudly, not knowing we were there.

"How could you possibly find that bear's den?"

Hearing Mack's voice, I caught Andrew's eye, and we both grew still, listening.

Jim said, "Helen's boy said it denned on that empty plot of land, the one that's been for sale for ages, out past the research cabin. Remember? At the trial? Two coffees, black please."

The cash register dinged and change rattled as the two men paid for their coffee. I shrank down in my chair, even though I knew they couldn't see me through the solid bookshelf.

Mack continued. "That plot is over a hundred acres. You're gonna find a bear den on a hundred acres? It's not worth it, Jim."

Jim made a sound somewhere between a grunt and a growl. "That bear charged me. What'll it take for people to see the danger—a kid getting attacked walking home from school?"

"Hey, I'm not arguing. The bear needs to go. But why not wait until spring?"

"With Helen breathing down our necks, fall will be here before we clear the red tape. Meanwhile, a dangerous bear is on the loose."

Chimes rang as they walked out of the shop.

"Patch." Andrew had whispered, his face drained of color. "I shouldn't have ... ..."

I cut him off, forcing my voice to be steady. "She'll be okay. We'll take care of her."

Now the forest was so quiet, I could almost hear the snow falling. Instead of making me feel calmer, the stillness amplified the worries inside my head. The family in Old Man Mueller's shack, so close to Patch. And the little girl, with her ungloved hands and her intense eyes, making me promise.

I hurried to catch up with Andrew. "I don't think we should tell anyone about that family."

"You never told us what she said." Andrew rubbed the red tip of his nose with his glove.

I swallowed hard. Even telling Ruth and Andrew felt like breaking my promise. The girl's dad hadn't seemed cruel, but his shotgun and hunting vest made me fear the girl's threat. "She said if I told anyone her family lives out here, she'd tell her dad the bears were near."

"So she might have seen the den?" Andrew started hiking again, his steps jerky and tense. "How could we be so careless? Why are they living out here? What are we going to do?"

"You should have seen her eyes, Andrew," I said. "If anyone asks about her family, she will bring her dad as close to the den as possible, I know she will. What will happen to Patch then?"

Andrew kept walking, but Ruth stopped and caught my arm. "Sadie …" As soon as I saw her pained expression, I heard my own words echo back to me. *We shouldn't tell.* These very words had led to a blow-out fight with Ruth less than a month ago, both because of the secret I asked Ruth to keep and the secret she kept from me. And it wasn't just Ruth. I had kept other secrets, wanting to handle problems without asking for help. Hadn't I learned anything at all?

Still, even though I knew Ruth was right, hot anger rose into my throat. "So what do you suggest, Ruth? We should tell? And leave Patch to fend for herself against that guy?"

"I didn't say …" Ruth began.

I turned away from her, not wanting the discussion to spiral into a fight. Andrew was far ahead, anyway, so I walked fast, pretending I only wanted to close the gap.

When I fell in step with Andrew, he said, "If we tell Mom about this, she'll take it all on herself. Whenever anything is serious, she entirely closes me out. I hate being treated like situations are too dangerous for me."

Andrew's reasons for hiding the truth matched mine: protecting his mom, protecting Patch, and not being treated like a kid. Still, over the past few months, secrets had proven to be ticking bombs. Hide them today, and tomorrow or the day after they'd blow up in your face.

"No matter what we do," I said slowly, hating my words even as I said them, "that little girl knows too much. We need your mom's help, Andrew. If we don't tell and that man ..."

During hunting season, Helen's favorite bear, Humphrey, had been shot. Dad and Helen had pulled the bear out of the bushes because she had to see the truth for herself. Even though Dad had avoided almost all of the details in his retelling, whenever I worried about Patch or one of the other bears, the scene flashed to mind as clear as if I had seen it myself. Humphrey sliding across the dirt, limp, lifeless. Instead of Helen bursting into tears, I was the one sobbing.

"I know," Andrew said as Ruth came up behind us.

She must have seen the apology in my eyes, because she smiled a small, sad smile.

When we unbuckled our snowshoes, Higgins jumped all over me, slowing down the process. I didn't mind, hoping Andrew would tell his mom before I finished. The whole thing—my promise, the little girl, the danger to Patch, the worry I knew Helen would feel—made Thanksgiving dinner turn to lead in my stomach. I walked inside, and the smell of pumpkin pie and turkey took my breath away, reminding me of how happy I had been just a few hours ago.

Ruth's family packed up to leave, but Ruth hung back to listen as we spoke with Helen.

"Sadie, you should probably explain," Andrew said.

So much for Andrew getting the worst over with. "Umm ..." I glanced over at Ruth, and then sighed. No matter how much I wished for one, no easy way to tell the story appeared. So I just told Helen what had happened, about the girl, her threat, and her family.

"I'll call Meredith over at the DNR and see if she'll hike out there with me tomorrow," Helen said. "If they're squatting, we may be able to remove them from the cabin."

"Isn't that up to the land company?" Andrew asked. "Like when Old Man Mueller stays out there?"

"What if they don't have any place else to live?" I surprised myself with my question. After the girl had threatened me, why did I care? "And what if the girl tells about Patch's den?"

"We'll figure it out." Helen shook her head and opened the file folder she held, turning back to Dad. "So, if I identify sows that might accept orphaned cubs and save the government thousands of dollars a year, then they won't turn down my research grant, right? If I'm saving them that kind of money?"

Ruth gave me a quick hug before running out to join her family, and I watched Helen talk to Dad. I couldn't look at Andrew. Just as he'd predicted, we had been shut out. Worse, somehow my explanation hadn't worked. How could Helen simply say, *we'll figure it out*, and go back to her other conversation? Didn't she understand about the shotgun and the little girl who might, even now, be showing Patch's den to her dad?

Choosing the right area of research was important, I knew, because every two years, Helen had to reapply for the grant that allowed her to research with the bears. This year, because the hunters were so mad, the DNR would be even more likely to turn down Helen's proposal. If she didn't renew the grant, she and Andrew would move out of the cabin by June, and Dad's job would be over then, too. Still, none of those problems felt as important as protecting Patch, right now in danger.

I finally looked over at Andrew, who clanked pots and pans too loudly as he scrubbed them in the sink. His lips were pressed together just like before when I teased him about his room. He kept his eyes down, not meeting mine. I wanted to grab the washcloth from his hands, fling it in his face, and shout that none of this was my fault. Instead, I joined Mom in the mudroom, barely holding in my frustration.

Mom handed me my scarf. "Thank goodness none of you kids were hurt. That family could have been dangerous."

They *were* dangerous. Didn't anyone understand?

"Hand me my boots, will you, Sades?" Mom sat on the bench and took off the house slippers Helen kept for visitors.

I passed her boots over and watched her lace them up, barely able to hold back the words I wanted to shout at everyone. Mom tied her last knot, stood, and pulled me into a puffy-coated hug. Her arms were strong, and through her coat, I couldn't feel her too thin shoulders. If I closed my eyes, this could almost be a hug from the past, back when Mom was truly herself. Why couldn't today have gone the way I planned and ended with this almost perfect hug?

"I love you, Sades," Mom said, and then let me go and pulled on her hat.

I shoved my feet into my boots as Dad came into the mudroom with Helen and Andrew. Higgins bounced along behind.

"I'll hike to the shack with you and Meredith tomorrow," Dad said to Helen. "I planned to drive Sadie out here anyway, so she can help finish with the promised clean up."

Miserable. After the worst ever Thanksgiving, now I would be forced to endure another day with Andrew in his current mood. Unhappiness kept me from looking at anyone as we said goodbye. I pulled Higgins into my lap and buried my nose in his fur so I wouldn't have to talk to my parents on the way home. Telling a secret before it blew up in my face was almost as difficult as waiting for the explosion.

Chapter 4

The List

I wrote *Dad* in purple pen across my clean sheet of printer paper and underlined his name in green. Amy Grant Christmas music played, Mom's favorite. The music reminded me of being three and four, decorating the tree, making cookies, squishing sand-dough into random shapes that I called a monkey or a snowman, which embarrassingly still hung on the tree every year. Christmas season had officially begun.

"Wish you were here, Pips." Homesickness panged sharp and sudden, and I realized just how much I missed Pips and my friends back in California. As long as I had known Pips, we had sat up into the late, late night on Thanksgiving, dreaming up our Christmas lists together.

The first time, when we were six, Pippa's parents had invited my family over for Thanksgiving dinner. All through the meal, Pips and I begged for a sleepover. My parents hesitated, remembering how homesick I had been on my last sleepover, so homesick they'd had to drive over in the middle of the night to bring me home. But I promised I wanted to stay, even when Mom looked me in the eye at the door and said, "Are you sure, Sadie?"

Pips and I had charged up the stairs to her room, and she let me wear her Strawberry Shortcake pajamas, which like everything Strawberry Shortcake had that magical strawberry smell. Or maybe that was just Pips' whole room, overflowing with Strawberry Shortcake characters, cars, houses, puff-stickers, and smelly pens.

Pips, in her pink striped flannel PJ's, climbed up onto her bed with those smelly pens and a spiral notebook. "Come up, Sadie." She patted the bed beside her. "Let's make a Christmas list. Not for us. Presents we'll give people. Okay?"

We made a list of gifts, complete with *trip to Australia to see the kangaroos* for her mom, and *helicopter-car* for my dad. Just like every other game of pretend that we played, we slipped entirely into the world of anything-was-possible and spun our elaborate plans.

After our pages were covered with red and green smelly swirls, we pushed the markers off the bed onto the floor, snuggled under the covers, and closed our eyes.

I couldn't sleep. Maybe because I was homesick, but mostly because that list, lying on the table next to me, had me worried. Helicopter cars didn't exist, and if they did, I obviously couldn't buy one.

"Sadie?" Pips whispered, her voice small and sad. "I can't really send my mom to Australia. I want to give my parents presents this year. Real presents. Not just something you make in school."

All my own worry faded. I had to help Pips. I sat up, fumbled for the lamp switch, and gathered the markers and the notebook.

"Then we'll give them real presents," I said, even though I had no idea how to do so.

I turned to a fresh page, and we brainstormed presents our parents could use. A calendar with pictures on each page. Stationary sets for our moms, with their names written in bright colors at the top of each page and on the envelope flaps. And my favorite idea, keychains made from metal nuts and washers strung on thick plastic laning.

With our lists finally done, we switched off the light and fell asleep almost before our heads hit the pillows. Even when Pips and I could buy presents with our allowance, we insisted on meaningful presents for everyone. No generic mugs full of candy from us.

On my updated list, Dad's name waited with nothing underneath. I wrote the names of my family and friends. Pips had asked for a drawing, back when I was taking art lessons. Maybe I could give her a drawing for Christmas. I opened the new sketchbook I hadn't been able to draw in since I'd stopped art lessons. I didn't know what to draw. Now I drew without thinking, tracing eyes, a mouth, a nose. My pencil stopped when I saw what I had drawn. The girl in the forest.

I ripped the page out and threw it in the trash. Without an assignment, my fingers seemed to have a mind of their own, and I didn't want to see what they would show me next. I needed a really good drawing assignment. Something to keep me from having to think. I powered on my computer and opened my email.

From: Sadie Douglas
To: Pippa Reynolds
Date: Thursday, November 25, 8:52 PM
Subject: Argggh

I miss drawing. Everything I draw turns out horrible, and I just want to toss it. I miss having a teacher, but I can't go back to Vivian. It's too weird. What should I do?

Sorry, that was a downer. BTW, Happy Thanksgiving. I started my Christmas list and missed you the whole time.

From: Sadie Douglas
To: Pippa Reynolds
Date: Thursday, November 25, 9:34 PM
Subject: Re: Re: Argggh

Thanks, Pips. I'm worried because Andrew is acting weird. He didn't want me to go in his room—what if he has a picture of a girl in there or something? It's not like we're going out together, as if my parents would even let me, and I don't even know if I like-like him. What am I going to do?

Going to the library and getting art books is a good idea. Vivian showed me some pictures by Van Gogh that I liked a lot. Maybe I'll look at his stuff.

Sorry about the caviar and starched linens. Why do parents always try to upgrade holidays? Don't they understand traditions? We had Thanksgiving in the research cabin this year. Not traditional, but we had all the right food, and everyone was there, and no one shouted when Hannah spilled mashed potatoes on the floor.

P.S. You've got me all excited. What present???!?

Chapter 5

Swirls and Dots

"Sades, phone for you." Dad tossed me the cordless phone. "And hurry up. I'm meeting Helen and Meredith at nine o-clock at the research cabin to hike out to the shack. We're late."

I held the phone to my ear. "Hello?"

Andrew sounded like he was shouting from the bottom of a cave.

"What?" Since I woke up, nervous thoughts about Andrew had built up like static electricity. Why was he calling now?

His voice came into focus. "Sorry, speaker phone. Look Sadie, I need the day off."

The static sparked, sharp and quick, like a shock when you touch metal. I tried to keep my voice level. "Dad's in a hurry. Can we talk when I get there?"

"No, I ... I need to work on stuff." He sounded rushed, not at all like himself.

"I know. That's what we're doing, cleaning the cabin." I had dressed in my oldest jeans and a hoodie with holes in the sleeves.

Dad had already pulled on his coat. "Sades, come on."

I pressed the phone between my shoulder and my ear and shoved my other arm into my coat. "Andrew, I need to go. I'll see you in a minute." I could deal with a little weirdness from him, especially since he would be at the cabin when Dad, Helen, and Meredith returned from their hike. After yesterday and what Helen said, listening in on conversations was probably the only way Andrew and I would get an update on the family in the wood.

"No, Sadie. Listen. You can't come today."

I stopped, letting my coat dangle off my shoulder. His words felt like a slap across the cheek. I *couldn't* come?

"Sadie—" Andrew said.

Weirdness was one thing, but going to the cabin after Andrew told me I couldn't was impossible. How could I face him now and act anything like normal?

I forced my voice to be light and said, "Sure. No problem. I need to ..." I grasped for something, anything I needed to do. "... go to the library anyway."

"Sadie—" Dad said.

I hung up before Andrew wasted breath on a fake apology.

"Sadie?" Dad tossed me my boots. "Time to go."

I ran upstairs to grab my sketchbook. The library? Now I

had to go, because otherwise I'd sit around home, acting as though I had no life unless I was with Andrew.

The entire drive to town, Dad lectured me about planning ahead for trips to the library and grumbled about being late for the hike with Meredith. His words were background noise compared to the mental tirade I carried on with Andrew. *I couldn't come out to the cabin?* After he had forced me to explain what happened in the woods, now he blamed me for Helen's reaction? Okay, everything's probably fine, but what's he hiding in his room anyway?

Sunlight reflected off the snow and streamed through the library's floor-to-ceiling windows. Light pooled on the burgundy carpet. Comfortable clumps of book-lined shelves created nooks and corners for armchairs with footstools, reading lamps, and end tables. Our high-tech library back in California was a library from a different universe. Here, on ordinary days, as soon as I walked in the door I wanted to bury my nose in a book. Today, though, I wondered if I'd be able to sit at all, with Helen, Meredith, and Dad on their way out to the shack, Patch totally unprotected in her den, and God knows what was up with Andrew.

I checked the clock. Nine fifteen, and Dad wasn't picking me up until one thirty. I took out my sketchbook. What would I draw if I opened to a blank page? The girl again, glaring at me because I'd broken my promise? Andrew frowning over the dishes? Or even worse, the girl's dad visiting Patch's den? Pips was right. I needed art books. I slung my backpack onto the floor and climbed onto one of three tall stools next to the catalog computers. The cursor flashed innocently, a silent question. *What would you like to find, Sadie?*

I wanted what I couldn't have. Vivian. My ex-art teacher, ever present, yet completely missing from my life. Every once in a while, I'd turn a corner and wham—her face appeared in my mind. The disappointed expression on her face at the trial where I'd testified against her son, Peter. Her intense gaze when she asked me to speak to Peter first, listen to his story, before I turned him in for shooting Big Murphy outside of hunting season. Sometimes I envisioned her happier, the way she smiled over my sketchbook after I completed a drawing, or when she lifted freshly baked cookies from the oven.

The cursor's question became louder with each blink. What did I want? What book could possibly make up for not having a teacher?

Vivian had shown me the painting *Starry Night*, and I'd liked the colors and the shapes, but mostly the feeling. Van Gogh. I typed his name, and the screen filled with titles.

Van Gogh and the Colors of the Night
Letters of Vincent Van Gogh
Van Gogh: Sunflowers and Swirly Stars

I scrolled back to the first title. *Van Gogh and the Colors of the Night*. *Starry Night* filled the cover. Sunflowers and landscapes in yellows and reds and greens on the other covers didn't appeal to me. I wasn't sure why, but the swirling blues and purples with the bright yellow starlight whispered of mystery.

I jotted the book's reference number on a slip of paper and wandered up and down rows of shelves. There were at least fifty art books. I pulled a few down, *The Art Book* and *50 Artists You Should Know*, and of course, the Van Gogh. I carried the pile to a nearby armchair.

Landscape after landscape filled *The Art Book*, including some of Van Gogh's paintings of flowers. Most, including Van Gogh's flowers, were too yellow, too finished. Creepy, lifeless eyes stared back at me from many of the portraits. I opened *50 Artists You Should Know*. More paintings I didn't love. I swallowed back guilt. Obviously someone smart thought these images were masterpieces. What was my problem? I flipped through the book again, more slowly now, trying to really look at the pictures. Picture after picture after picture. Frustrated, I closed the book and returned to *Starry Night*. The difference startled me. My eyes slipped along the curve of the blue toward the crescent moon and then tumbled from star to star down into the quiet town. Questions popped up, unexpected. Who slept here? What went on in the houses with lit windows? An idea flickered at the edge of my mind, but I couldn't put it into words. I opened *The Art Book* again to one of the first images, *The Nubian Giraffe*.

In the picture, a giraffe stood near two Arab keepers and a gentleman in a suit. The giraffe's head hovered above the three men who were deep in conversation. If I thought about it, I could list all sorts of questions about this painting. And yet, questions didn't spring to mind naturally.

Was this the difference? *Starry Night* invited me to wonder, but many of the other pictures did not. Paintings — captured still moments — couldn't help but feel finished. And yet, the way my eyes moved around *Starry Night* made me feel as though time could pass, as though my own ideas and thoughts about the scene mattered, making the picture more than just a picture.

Looking at books was nothing like going to Vivian's house. Vivian would ask me questions, give me an assignment. What was my assignment now? Vivian would tell me to look carefully. To draw what I saw. Would drawing *Starry Night* teach me something?

I slid my colored pencils out of my bag, set the Van Gogh book on the end table, and tried to draw there in my sketchbook. My pencils rolled off the little table, and my elbows bumped into the armrests. After struggling for a few minutes, I packed everything up and headed for the larger table at the back of the library.

I rounded the last shelf and stopped. The last person I expected sat at the end of the long table. Frankie.

Chapter 6

Illusion

Not the Frankie who had left two weeks ago, though. At first, I couldn't pinpoint the exact difference. Her white blond hair was pulled back in her usual ponytail, but she clearly had a new, layered haircut. Strands fell around her chin, framing her face, which was different, too. Her eyebrows were thinner, more arched. Her eyelashes were darker, and small crystals sparkled like stars in her newly pierced ears. Her fingernails weren't cherry red with chipped edges. Instead of being painted, now they shone. Frankie had always been pretty, but now she looked ...... what was the word? Finished? Like a sketch that had been detailed into a final drawing.

Strangest of all, her expression was wrong. When she looked up at me, the edge of her mouth tilted up slightly before she returned to her drawing. No sharp insult. No fierce glare. What did that odd expression — could you call it a smile — mean? And why, after being gone for so long, was she sitting in the library with her math book?

I had two options: sit down and draw or leave. For reasons I couldn't understand, leaving seemed wrong. Mean, somehow. Not that Frankie had wanted me anywhere near before. But something about her drooping shoulders made me feel that walking away would be cruel.

So I sat down, took out my pencils, and tried to draw.

But I couldn't. Not with Frankie at the end of the table — probably watching and dreaming up more insults about me existing on the planet. After three false starts, I finally sketched the shape of the swirls in the sky, the curve of the moon. Every once in a while, I looked up at Frankie. She kept her eyes down, black ink covering her page. Her image wasn't really a drawing, more a random collection of lines. I'd never seen Frankie draw. I'd never seen Frankie without a group of friends nearby.

I shouldn't stare.

I forced my attention back to my drawing, to the big, blue-black shape in *Starry Night* — the mountain or bush or what was it? I sketched the outline and started shading it in.

"Do you understand this order of operations thing?"

Frankie had turned to a fresh page in her notebook and written an equation at the top. I blinked at her, hearing her words repeat two or three times in my mind before I comprehended what she had asked. She had not insulted me. She had asked me a question. About math.

"I'm interrupting you." She waved her hand in the air, as though she was batting her question away, out of the space between us.

I turned back to my drawing. What should I do? I was no math whiz myself. But I had finally, after hours of struggling, figured out the order of operations. Frankie made an x through her first attempt and wrote the equation again. I slid down the bench until I sat across from her.

After watching Frankie write and erase numbers for a while, I finally gathered the courage to say, "The part that confused me was doing the multiplication and division first, and then the addition and subtraction."

"You don't have to help me, Sadie."

There. The sharp tone I expected from Frankie. But still, no sarcasm, no evil glare. And really, did I wish the torture of learning the order of operations on anyone—even Frankie?

"I don't mind."

She looked up and smiled that tiny almost smile again. "Truly?"

She tore a page out of her notebook and passed it over. I wrote the equation.

"First do everything in the parenthesis. You already had that. And then any multiplication or division, left to right. Last, do the addition or subtraction." I handed the page back.

Instead of looking at the numbers, she studied me. "What are you drawing?"

I shrugged. "*Starry Night*. Van Gogh."

"Do you still take art lessons?"

At first I wondered how she knew these things, but then I remembered my presentation at school, in October, with all my drawings. I must have said something then. I wouldn't have thought Frankie would remember anything about me, unless it was fuel for a new insult.

"No."

"I think Vivian Harris should come back to our classroom. To do more art with us, I mean. All we ever do is math and science and English and social studies. And PE. Running. My favorite." Her sarcasm was back.

"Mine too."

I was smiling at Frankie. Frankie, who had hated me before she even met me because of my dad's job. Frankie, whose dad, at this very moment, was plotting to shoot Patch as she slept in her den, and in a flash all my worries flooded back. I checked the clock. Noon. Dad, Helen, and Meredith were probably with the family in the woods right now, unless they had already left.

I slid back to my seat and quickly packed up my pencils and notebook. "I'll see you around."

"See ya." Frankie went back to her math.

At the main desk, I checked out the Van Gogh, and the librarian convinced me to borrow a book she'd just bought, *Masters of Deception*. Its pages revealed illusion after optical illusion, arches that turned out to be boats on a sea, a photograph of a heap of bottles and shakers that cast the shadow of a woman with an umbrella.

I stood and flipped through the astonishing images, but even they couldn't hold my attention. Dad wouldn't be here for another hour and a half, but my legs were jumpy and I had to get some fresh air. After I packed up my bag and bundled up, I went outside. Even in my coat, hat, and boots, the fifteen-degree air wouldn't allow me to take the walk I needed so badly. But after my awkward conversation with Frankie, I couldn't go back into the library. Time for hot chocolate at Black Bear Java.

From: Sadie Douglas
To: Pippa Reynolds
Date: Friday, November 26, 8:15 PM
Subject: Snirt...

Snirt is officially known as dirt-snow that sits around and gets trampled and driven all over. Or so I learned today at Black Bear Java from Ben, this old guy who goes to Black Bear every day for lunch and a crossword puzzle. I had the weirdest possible conversation with Frankie. She was almost nice, Pips. What does that mean?

Dad, Helen, and Meredith hiked out to see the family in the cabin in the woods, and apparently the cabin is all fixed up on the inside, with furniture and everything. Some person — the man and his wife wouldn't say who — is purchasing the land and giving them the cabin. Helen called the land company and the story checks out. Helen prodded for information about the bear, but no one said anything about Patch's den. Dad says no one can stop the family from living there, and I have no answers about why the little girl made me promise not to tell about them. Patch is still in trouble. But Helen, Dad, and Meredith say we have to let it go. How am I supposed to let it go?

From: Sadie Douglas
To: Pippa Reynolds, Juliet Chance, Alice Cheng, Brianna Ingles
Date: Saturday, November 27, 8:27 PM
Subject: Re: Christmas Shopping

I'm so so so jealous. Shopping in downtown San Francisco on Thanksgiving weekend is the best. Thanks for sending me the pictures of the lights and the kittens in Macy's window. And you're all spending the night in the St. Regis, too. Lucky ducks.

From: Sadie Douglas
To: Pippa Reynolds
Date: Sunday, November 28, 5:15 PM
Subject: Too quiet

Still no word on Patch, and Dad keeps telling me not to worry. As though it were a switch you could just turn off.

Chapter 7

Traditions

On Monday morning, Frankie's desk was empty. The old radiator clanked and spewed hot, dusty air into the classroom. Bright light shone through the paned windows, but still I felt shut in, itchy. Andrew and I hadn't talked since Friday's phone conversation. The little girl's face haunted my thoughts. Why did she want me to promise not to tell anyone about her if her family hadn't done anything wrong? If I could just hike to the cabin, convince the girl to keep Patch's den a secret. How much does she really know?

Ruth shot me a silent question, looking meaningfully at Frankie's empty desk— *Where is she?* I shrugged. Who knew?

Ms. Murphy was more flustered than ever. Her hair frizzed out of her messy bun, and her glasses hung lopsided on their beaded chain. She flipped through one file after another, taking out one paper here, another there. She made me feel nervous just looking at her. I stacked and restacked my textbooks.

"See the rock on her finger?" Abby whispered to Erin, loud enough for the class to hear.

Abby and Erin each shared an earphone from their iPod, like they did every morning. The music was so loud I could hear it three rows over.

For the first time that year, the class fell dead silent, all eyes front. Ms. Murphy looked down at her hand.

"Welcome back from the long weekend." She cleared her throat. "As Abby and Erin have noticed, I had a surprise over Thanksgiving break."

Ms. Murphy held up her hand to show off the sapphire on her ring finger, and then smiled, a very shy, strange smile for a teacher. "I'm engaged."

Everyone started talking, and a few boys wolf-whistled. Ms. Murphy's smile didn't fade. Finally, she held up both hands for quiet.

"Okay. It's out in the open and over. That's enough. We're starting a new project today with partners, and I need your attention."

Chairs scraped across the scratched linoleum as students stood and scrambled toward the partner of their choice. The door banged open, interrupting the process, and Frankie walked in, her face stony. She looked way different. Though she tried to disguise her haircut with loads of gel and a pony-tail, no one could miss the pierced ears or designer jeans — even with rips in the knees.

"Look who decided to show up," Ty said. He had to make his presence known, having just returned from a prolonged suspension. He smirked at his cronies, Mario, Dmitri, and Nick. "Miss New York fashion herself."

I caught Ruth's eye. She looked surprised, too. Frankie flushed. Ty's harsh tone towards Frankie was quite different than his usual flirty sappiness. And what did he mean about New York? Nicole and Tess, Frankie's friends, both stared at their fingernails. Frankie didn't have an ounce of Saturday's sadness. Now, her perfectly shaped eyebrows lifted, daring anyone and everyone. She held Ty's gaze for a long moment. Ms. Murphy watched their exchange, but didn't give the traditional tardy speech.

"Everyone take a seat. You will not choose your own partners. Write your name and toss it in the basket." Groans filled the room, Frankie and Ty forgotten, and Ms. Murphy ignored our grumbling as she collected our assorted slips of paper. When that was done, she started the picking process, row by row, Abby first.

Abby drew Ty's name and her cheeks flamed. The back-row boys made kissing sounds. Unfortunately for Abby, everyone knew she had a crush on Ty. I watched Frankie for signs of irritation, but other than one raised eyebrow, Frankie didn't flinch. Nicole drew Tess. Ruth got Mario. Then me. I opened my slip. Not possible. Frankie.

"Since it's December, we'll combine our survey of world religions with the study of holiday traditions. Each group will fully research their topic, write a paper, and make a presentation to the class."

More grumbling.

"Our purpose in this project is to explore how religion affects culture. Pair up."

Ms. Murphy passed out envelopes as we dragged our desks next to our partners. I carried my books to the desk next to Frankie's. Obviously, she had no intention of moving.

"You want to open the envelope?" I asked.

She shrugged. "Whatever. You do it."

I was so unsure with Frankie. Had our talk at the library changed things between us? I waited until Ms. Murphy distributed all the other packets.

"I said open it," Frankie said.

I sighed, ripped it open, and took out our assignment. "St. Lucia Day, Sweden." Never heard of it.

Ms. Murphy glanced at our assignment and placed a thick packet on my desk. Back at the board, she said, "Both partners are responsible for equal amounts of research. Your packet's first page lists the research categories. Divide the categories between you and your partner, label your topics with your name, and turn the page in before you leave for PE."

Perfect. Now Frankie and I had to have a discussion.

Frankie dug her pen into her desktop. "I'll do food, activities, and cultural importance of the tradition. And the overview of current Sweden. You do the religious stuff. You're all churchy with Ruth, aren't you?"

Was I? I rolled the word around in my mind. Churchy. A word that wrinkles your nose and feels like it should be hidden in your most private drawer. Before I met Ruth, before

I visited her youth group, before I found myself looking for answers in an empty church on a stormy night, I would have cringed to hear anyone describe me this way. But now, the word bothered me for different reasons. After I curled up in that quiet sanctuary, when the warmth of something unimaginable and yet undeniably real wrapped around me, I could no longer doubt that God existed, and more importantly, that he cared. Churchy was such a small word, the absolute wrong word. My experience had nothing to do with buildings, whatever churchy was.

But I didn't feel like arguing with Frankie. I wrote her name next to the topics she'd chosen and my name next to the others. I pried the staple off the packet, ripping my fingernail in the process, but freed the cover sheet and took it up to Ms. Murphy.

"You and Frankie decided quickly." Ms. Murphy squinted at me over the top of her glasses. "Will you two work together all right?"

Translation: Frankie frequently insults you and has hated you since she moved here until she unexpectedly disappeared for two weeks, had some kind of makeover that she's trying to hide, and now she doesn't seem to be talking to anyone, including her friends, so please make this work, Sadie.

"Sure. No problem." I said. I smiled and returned to my desk.

I flipped through *Masters of Deception,* silently rehearsing what I might say to the girl in the woods. Would seeing me again make her more angry?

Finally the bell rang. Ruth was deep in argument with Mario. I walked to PE without her, but she barreled into me by my locker.

"Mario hates me, Sadie. And he won't do anything. He wrote his name down for food. Food. He refuses to do anything else. Ms. Murphy finally told us to give her our choices tomorrow. We got Hanukkah."

I told her about Frankie as we swiveled our padlocks and opened our lockers. Stale gym clothes smell wafted out. I fished out my gym shirt. "Gross. I need to wash these clothes. How can I sweat when it's like ten degrees outside?"

"Weather says that it actually *will* be ten degrees. An arctic chill is on the way."

"Perfect. How do people survive this cold?" How did the family in the woods manage in a house with no electricity or heat?

Girls hurried past on their way outside, their hats pulled low over their ears. Ruth and I were the last girls left. As Ruth finished pulling on her thermal pants, I said, "I want to snowshoe to the shack again to talk to that girl. I want to convince her not to tell about Patch."

Ruth stopped. "What if the family is dangerous?"

"Helen and Dad didn't think so. They met the family. They're convinced the man's safe. They aren't worried."

"But you're worried." Ruth finished tying her boot.

"About Patch. Please, Ruth. Will you come with me?"

"Ladies?" Mr. Tyree thumped on the locker room door and called loudly. "We're waiting."

Ruth slipped her ear warmers over her ears. "Okay. I'll go with you." She shook her head. "How do you get me into these situations?"

I grinned at her, grabbed my gloves and hat, and we hurried outside to freeze.

From: Sadie Douglas
To: Pippa Reynolds, Juliet Chance, Alice Cheng, Brianna Ingles
Date: Monday, November 29, 7:55 PM
Subject: In Michigan, in the winter, DO NOT...

Volunteer to retrieve the soccer ball from the snow bank in PE. The snowbank is deeper than you think.

Go outside with earrings in. You get instant cold-headache from frozen metal in your ears.

Let your parents convince you to walk the dog after you've washed your hair. Hair freezes.

From: Sadie Douglas
To: Pippa Reynolds
Date: Tuesday, November 30, 9:24 PM
Subject: GRRRRRRR

Higgins won't stop biting my pencil as I draw, and when I make him get off the bed, he barks nonstop. And I can't make my drawings look like the ones in the book, no matter how many times I redraw them. I miss Vivian.

Chapter 8

Pieces

Sand caked my bare feet. Pips and I smoothed the sides of our ten-story sandcastle, complete with turrets and moat, when horses covered with jingle bells pulled a sleigh onto the beach. The driver, a woman in a poison green velvet coat, waved us over. I caught Pippa's eye — should we trust this woman? The moment faded, the way dreams do, dissolving into cold morning air, colder than usual. Bells jingled outside my open window. Wait a minute ... I sat up. The jingling bells didn't go away. Who had opened my window? I shivered and pulled the covers tight.

Higgins, asleep at the end of the bed, groaned and rolled over. I slipped on my fuzzy purple slippers and brought the comforter with me as I peeked out the window.

Nothing. The bells faded into the woods on the far side of the house. I flipped my trailing comforter over my arm like the train of an enormous wedding dress and stumbled downstairs. Higgins bounced close at my heels, awake now, ready to be part of the fun.

"Strange sounds outside this morning, Sadie," Dad called from the kitchen.

Pancakes sizzled, and the vanilla-sweet smell of baking batter wafted into the living room.

"What's going on?"

"I don't know. You'd better go look."

I rolled my eyes. Dad loved to play this game. He absolutely knew what was happening outside. I ran my fingers through my hair, just in case, and threw open the door. Higgins burst outside and stopped to sniff, instantly entering his hunting mode.

He circled the rectangular box on the porch, sniffing every angle of the shiny red and green striped paper, the red velvet bow on top, and the tag labeled *Sadie*. He cocked his head at me. I looked out toward the forest but couldn't see anyone.

"What is this?" I called to Dad.

"What?" he asked, innocently, as if he was clueless.

"Come on, Higgy." I gritted my teeth against the cold, tossed the comforter back into the living room and shivered in my pajamas as I picked up the heavier-than-expected box. I kicked the door shut behind me and carried the box to the kitchen table.

"You're telling me this isn't from you?" I asked Dad.

He shrugged, but didn't turn from the stove.

"Should I open it?"

"It's got your name on it."

"See! How did you know that? You didn't even look."
Still, after Pips had told me about her bigger-than-spectacular
present for me this year, I knew this must be from her.

Dad grinned. He wore the ruffled pink apron he had
worn on the first day in our new house. It said *Sugar and
Spice and Everything Nice*. Someone had given the apron to
Mom back in California, and it had been the only apron
Dad could find when we unpacked. Now he wore it every
time he cooked. I had tried everything, ignoring the apron,
teasing him about the apron, looking pointedly at the apron.
Nothing worked. The joke was funnier to him every single
time.

Holding my breath, I ripped into the paper. The box was
big enough to hold almost anything. Bigger than a book.
Bigger than a sweater. Higgins put his paws up on the table
and nosed my hand as I pulled tissue out of the box.

"No, Higgins, this isn't for you."

I lifted the painted wooden tree out and set it on the
table. Small drawers, each painted with a picture of a bright
ornament, numbered from one to twenty four. The tree was
painted dark green and textured with lighter and darker
greens, giving it a three-dimensional look.

"Dad, I didn't know you painted. Or made stuff with
wood. When did you ..."

"Who says I built this?" Dad came over to look more
closely. "Excellent woodsmanship."

He hurried back to the stove to flip pancakes onto plates. "Oh, come on, Dad."

I hadn't had an advent calendar since I was very young, maybe four or five, and then only the paper kind where you open a door to a new picture each day.

"Are you going to open number one?" Dad asked.

Today was December first. I pulled open the drawer.

Inside sat a yellow origami star. A label along one edge read *Open Me*.

I turned the star over in my hands. "It's so cute. I don't want to pull it apart."

"Choices," Dad said. "Why don't you take your box upstairs and call Mom for breakfast."

I closed the star back in the drawer. Maybe I would open the star later today. If the advent calendar was from Pips, who had rung the bells? I didn't recognize the handwriting— carefully neutral block letters. As far as I knew, neither Mom nor Dad knew how to paint or fold origami. Pips knew that I'd love not knowing, too.

I tossed my comforter over the box and headed for the stairs. Higgins did his best to try to trip me all the way upstairs. After depositing my comforter and the box in my bedroom, I went to wake Mom.

"Breakfast!" I called, not daring to open the door. Even before she got sick, Mom had never been a morning person. She needed large amounts of coffee and an ocean of personal space to move from the land of sleep into the land of the awake.

I took the stairs two at a time, skidded back into the kitchen, and sat across from Dad. Higgins put his chin on my lap and looked up with huge, pathetic eyes. Maple syrup already dripped off the edges of Dad's pancakes.

"Oh, fine, Higgy. Breakfast for you first."

As I filled Higgins' bowl, I watched snow fall outside the window, filling the disappearing footprints that led out toward the trees. Footprints. Dad had stood a foot from this window, flipping pancakes, so he had to have seen the bell ringer.

I sat back down and doused my pancakes with syrup. "So, who rang those bells?"

"Beats me," Dad shoved a big bite into his mouth.

"Right." I couldn't fight the lure of the pancakes. Dad would eventually crack, admit he had asked someone to ring the bells for Pippa. Or could she be here? But that wasn't possible. If Pips were here, she'd be here at our house with us. No present or grand scheme would keep her from actually coming to see me after three months of being apart.

After a few minutes of pure pancake bliss, Dad nodded at the thermometer outside the kitchen window, which read one degree. "Cold this morning. The roads are icy, so we need to leave a little early. Can you be ready in fifteen minutes?"

"Sure." I'd perfected the art of getting ready quickly.

"And take some coffee up to Mom, will you? I'll wash up."

I poured a mug of coffee and took it upstairs. "Mom?"

"Mmmm." She rolled over in bed and reached out for the mug, her eyes still closed.

I put the mug in her hands. "Love you."

Part of getting ready quickly was planning ahead. While I ran down the hall to my bedroom, I chose my outfit. Soft, red sweater. Jeans. Fur-lined boots. I quickly made my bed and closed the window. No way was I changing with icy air blowing in. Other than Dad, who could have opened my window? Even if the tree was from Pips, Dad was in on it too. No question.

After I dressed, I grabbed my backpack. On the way out the door, I opened drawer number one and slipped the star into my pocket.

The heater blasted in the Jeep. I climbed in, and gradually my body temperature climbed higher and higher.

"Okay. Heat off." In coat, hat, and gloves, too much heat made the Jeep feel like a sauna.

When we pulled up to school, I kissed Dad's cheek.

"Happy first of December, Sadie," he said.

"You too, Dad. Thanks for the surprise this morning."

"I'm telling you —"

"It's not from you." I finished with him.

Chapter 9

Secrets

Ms. Barton had booked the town library for the morning so we had access to more research for our reports. For most of the first hour, I gathered books about St. Lucia Day, taking twice as long as I needed because I was preoccupied with my present. Finally, I sat next to Ruth, who grumbled through an oversized book on Israel.

"He still hasn't agreed to do anything but food. Look at him." Ruth nodded toward the table of guys: Ty, Mario, Dmitri.

None of the guys even pretended to look at books. Instead, they folded paper airplanes and tossed them at Nicole and Tess. Ms. Barton pursed her lips and walked toward their table.

I put my hand on Ruth's book. "Ruth, jingle bells woke me up this morning. And I found an advent calendar wrapped on my porch. It's a really cool wooden Christmas tree with drawers for each day."

"No way. From who?"

"I don't know. Pips told me my present would be extra special this year, but she couldn't have pulled off the bells without Dad's help."

Ruth closed her book with a thump. "Did you open the first day?"

"Yes. This was inside." I handed over the star.

"Working, ladies?" Ms. Barton asked, passing by our table.

I stuffed the star back into my pocket and opened the top book on my stack. *Scholars have no common agreement on the exact beginnings of St. Lucia Day. Though the holiday has become culturally important in Sweden, it may have begun in Germany.*

"If the holiday isn't just a Swedish holiday, why does she want us to study Sweden?" I closed the book and opened the next.

"Listen." Ruth looked up at Ms. Barton, who stood close enough to our table that I couldn't take the star back out safely.

Ruth read from her book. "*Hanukkah is an important Jewish holiday, but it is not a holy day. On holy days, all work ceases. Holy days are set apart. Hanukkah is considered a festival day, a celebration, but Jewish people are still allowed to go to work and school.*"

I whispered, hoping Ms. Barton wouldn't hear. "So why are we wasting our time?"

"Whoa." Frankie slid onto the bench next to me, and pointed at the pictures in my book. A parade of girls in white dresses carried candles through city streets, and a close up showed a girl wearing a wreath of lit candles on her head. "Why doesn't her hair catch on fire?"

Ruth stiffened, on guard. I didn't blame her. Before, when Frankie single-mindedly aimed to ruin our lives, we knew what to expect. Now, anything was possible.

"I found some information on Swedish food and on the celebration itself." Frankie piled her books on top of mine and opened a notebook.

We worked for a while, strangely, in silence. In the quiet, thoughts of Patch slipped into my mind. When would Ruth and I hike out to the cabin?

Ruth elbowed me again. "Sadie, help me find a book."

I followed her to the shelf.

"What's going on with Frankie?" Ruth asked.

I shrugged. Why hadn't I told Ruth about Frankie and the library on Saturday? What was going on with me?

Ruth flipped through a book as Ms. Barton walked by. "I don't trust her. Frankie wouldn't be nice to you or me unless she wanted something."

"Come on, Ruth." To be honest, though, I had already thought the same thing. "I don't know," I said, shaking my head. "But when are we hiking to the shack?"

"This weekend maybe, if it's not too cold. Will Helen really let us?"

"Maybe Andrew can work it out for us." Andrew. Another sore subject. But the weekend seemed too far away.

Frankie looked up and frowned. I knew she couldn't hear us, but she couldn't miss our heads together, whispering.

"Let's go back. I don't want Frankie to think we're talking about her."

Ruth glanced over her shoulder before sliding the book back onto the shelf. "Okay, but first let's see that star."

I took out the star and pulled the small folded tab. When I smoothed out the paper, I saw that the decorative marks had meaning—part of a path, maybe, and a couple letters. As though this was part of . . .

"A map," Ruth whispered, her words echoing my thoughts. "If it were me, I'd open every drawer tonight, and put it all together."

But I wouldn't. There were two letters, DR, and a line that looked like a path. I glanced up at Ruth sharply, a sudden thought shaking my confidence that the calendar was from Pips.

"Ruth, is the calendar from you?"

Ruth grinned and shook her head. "Maybe it's from Andrew."

Andrew hadn't crossed my mind. No way. Andrew wasn't even speaking to me. He never would have made me a present like this.

From: Sadie Douglas
To: Pippa Reynolds
Date: Wednesday, December 1, 9:23 PM
Subject: St. Francis

I found a new prayer that I like in the Book of Common Prayer.
My favorite part is the first line: Lord, make us instruments of
your peace. I picture myself becoming a viola or a cello, playing
peaceful music, instead of what I am now ... a loud, rackety
mess.

One very good thing happened today, though. Pips, I think
your present arrived today, the very, very, very most wonderful
present ever. I won't ask you to tell me if this IS your present,
because I know you love surprising me. But now, what will I
give you?

Chapter 10

Deception

The minute my eyes opened the next morning, I ran for the advent calendar. Trying to conserve body heat, I vaulted back into bed and tossed the covers over my legs. Higgins flopped down next to me and put his head on my lap with an enormous dog sigh. I scratched his ears.

A round ornament had been painted on drawer two, white with a red stripe around the middle. The careful painting wasn't terribly difficult. Now that Ruth had asked about Andrew, I couldn't be sure, one hundred percent, that the calendar was from Pips. Andrew? Again, the thought made me dizzy. I shoved the wish that Andrew made the calendar deep, deep down.

An origami boat, its base colored blue, sat inside drawer two. Even though the boat didn't have an *Open Me* label, I smoothed it open. Another section of map. I took the star out of my bedside table drawer and lay it next to the boat, moving them so their sides touched in every possible variation. These two pieces didn't go together. I didn't mind the wait. The longer the wait, the better the surprise.

I got ready on autopilot, using most of my brain to think about the calendar. I tried not to worry about Patch. Hopefully, Dad would take me and Ruth to the research cabin this weekend. Over cereal, I asked Dad about yesterday's footprints, but he didn't crack, not even a little.

The only thing that got me through the school day was looking forward to youth group that night. Mom had promised to take me and Ruth to dinner in Hiawatha, the next town over, a rare treat. So when Mom pulled up at school to pick me up, her faced lined with pain, I wanted to kick the car tires. Mom wouldn't go anywhere tonight.

"I'm sorry, Sades," Mom said, as soon as I opened the door.

"It's okay, Mom." I meant it and didn't mean it at the same time.

We didn't talk much on the way home. Mom needed all of her strength to drive through the snow safely. And I couldn't figure out a single thing to say that wasn't a lie, or just plain dumb. *You'll feel better soon* had become empty words. Words to express a wish we both knew was as likely as turning invisible or learning to fly.

After helping her back to bed, I clipped a leash to Higgy's collar and shivered on our two laps around the house. Higgins was a good dog, but not good enough to be trusted outside without a leash. I needed to call Ruth to cancel plans, but when I came in from the cold I just wanted to lie on my bed.

I lay there, counting knots on the log ceiling, trying not to think about Mom, about how I wished she would fight the disease harder, even when I knew nothing helped. Still, I needed her, and my need filled me with guilt. I needed her for what, to take me out to dinner? She was miserable and sick and all I could think about was my ruined plan?

Higgins padded up the stairs and stood by my bed, eyeing me.

"I know, Higgy. I need to call Ruth. And Dad."

Higgins nosed my arm. I rubbed his velvety ear between my fingers.

"Okay." I dragged myself up and went to the phone.

Dad would come home as soon as he could. Ruth's mom couldn't take us to dinner, but she would drive us over to youth group.

I did my homework, made myself a peanut butter and Doritos sandwich, and then flipped open *Masters of Deception* to the M.C. Escher chapter. The first image, *Day and Night*, showed a daytime landscape blending into an identical nighttime scene. In the middle of the picture, the birds looked black with white sky around them, but when I closed my eyes and reopened them, the birds became white against black sky.

Page after page showed these patterns that forced me to look again, but still, like many of the pictures in *The Art*

Book, I wasn't tempted to draw any of Escher's work. That is, until I turned the page and saw *Drawing Hands*. I took out my sketchbook and pencils. Escher had drawn hands that seemed to rise out of the page and draw themselves.

I traced the lines with my eyes, looking more at the book than at my drawing. If I thought too hard, my mind would convince me the angles were off. After all, I could hardly accept the picture in the first place. Three dimensional hands couldn't be two dimensional at the same time.

I stepped away from my drawing to take a better look. Certainly not as convincing an illusion as Escher's, but still intriguing. Why did the picture hold my attention so completely? As I struggled to see both realities, the mix of images, the clattering thoughts of the past few days became quieter. I turned back to the book and flipped the page to the Ron Gonsalves chapter titled Magical Realism. On each page, a picture showed one scene and another. Contradictions.

Pay attention. Look here.

I would have missed the whispering voice, had it not been for the calm focus that came along with the words, like the quiet after a storm.

I slowed, trying to truly see the images. Light spilled from the pages. Reality bent. Two boys rode down a leaf-lined street that was also treetops for a street below. People ran stocking-footed down a road, carrying mirrors that blended together into what looked like a river running between buildings. When I reached the chapter's end, I riffled back to the beginning and began to sketch. Maybe if I took time with these pictures, drew them with my own hands, I could climb inside them and understand how two contradictory things could be true. Why did the need to understand this impossibility burn against my wall of doubt? Face after face flashed in my mind. Frankie, Mom, Andrew, the girl in the woods, and finally me. *What am I supposed to see?*

And then the moment passed, and I still didn't have any answers. I felt like I'd struggled through a thick fog toward a lighted doorway, and when I finally made it across the room, the door slammed, leaving me lost and blind in the darkness. I laid my forehead down on the desk and squeezed my eyes shut, hoping Ruth's mom would come soon.

Chapter 11

A Christmas Project

Every time I crossed the church's back field, I stopped for a minute to take it all in: the treehouse with its turrets and weathervanes and wind chimes. Climbing up the rope ladder had been treacherous since the snow had started. Tonight, my boots slipped and slid on the frozen rungs. Still, when Doug asked, our group voted unanimously to meet in the treehouse through the winter, despite the challenges. Youth group wouldn't be the same in a church classroom. Usually on the first Thursday of a month, we'd be off for an outdoor adventure, but for December, Doug had announced the schedule would be different.

Penny muscled Ruth and I onto the deck. A few weeks ago, Doug had thanked Penny for power blowing snow off the treehouse porch every other day. Apparently, even with the strong supports, too much snow could break the porch off the side of the building.

Penny wore a Santa hat over her spiky teal-tipped hair. Cold reddened her nose and cheeks, but she gave us her usual grin. "Turn around!"

She taped papers to each of our backs. "Head on in. The space heaters are blasting, there's fresh baked chocolate chip cookies, and you have five minutes to figure out whose name is on your back. Yes or no questions only. Famous people. Have fun!"

Inside the treehouse, most people roamed from window-seat to windowseat, asking questions. A few of the younger boys body slammed one another with pillows, and the band members checked microphones and guitar amps. Ruth and I headed directly for the cookies.

She groaned. "I'm terrible at this game. I'll bet you fifty bucks I don't even know my person. I have no popular culture."

I checked the slip on her back. *Abe Lincoln.* "Sure, I'll bet you. I could use fifty bucks for Christmas shopping."

The hot, gooey cookies fell open onto our napkins as soon as we took bites.

I licked chocolate off my lips. "So who is mine? A man?"

"No."

Lindsay and Bea, the only other youth group girls our age, joined us at the cookie table.

"I already guessed mine," Lindsay said. "But Bea can't figure hers out."

"Is mine a singer?" Ruth asked Lindsay.

"No."

"A dancer?"

Lindsay caught my eye, and we both doubled over with laughter as we imagined Abe Lincoln dancing, with his top hat wobbling on the top of his tall, pole-like body.

"What?" Ruth asked.

Three questions later, I knew who I was. "Beyonce?"

"Yes!" Lindsay and Bea shouted.

Ruth still hadn't figured out her character by the time Doug asked us all to sit down. We pulled the names off our backs, and Ruth rolled her eyes.

"You didn't tell me he was a president."

"You owe me fifty bucks."

We settled into the regular routine. Doug prayed, the youth group band—Equilibrium—played, and people sang along. Cameron, the lead singer of the band and an eighth grader at our school, had been friends with Ruth since mid-fall. Everyone put extra emphasis on the word friends, which irritated Ruth, but she couldn't hide the smile that crept across her face every time she saw him. I teased Ruth about Cameron, but honestly, I liked they way they acted around each other, comfortable, like best friends. The way Andrew and I used to be. Andrew. Every time I thought about him, I wanted to hide under a rock.

When the band finished their set, Doug headed to the front. "So, it's December. Penny, Ben, and I decided to let you decide how we should celebrate Christmas. Thoughts?"

"Pizza party!" Ted played football for Hiawatha High and seemed to think only about two things—food and football.

Bea raised her hand. "Secret Santa? You know, where you pick someone's name and give secret presents and everyone tries to guess who their Santa is until the end when we find out?"

Jasper, the youngest member of our group, called out, "We could do one of those living nativity things, where you stand in costume and ..."

"Freeze in the snow?" Ted asked. "No, thank you."

"It's better than eating pizza for Christmas," Claudia said, in a rare moment of standing up for Jasper. Usually she couldn't wait to pounce on his suggestions.

"All right," Doug said. "Let's back up a second. Before we decide the particulars, let's toss out thoughts on what we all want from a Christmas celebration, here as a group."

"Not just a party," Lindsay said. "We should do something for someone else."

"In elementary school, our Sunday school teacher gave us shoeboxes that we filled with toothbrushes and shoelaces and combs and toys, and sent them to kids in Africa," Claudia said.

"I ..." Jasper frowned and broke off.

"What are you thinking, Jasper?" Doug asked.

"Well it sounds bad, I guess, but why don't we help people around here? People we can see? Not that I don't think kids in Africa need stuff, but ..."

"Oh!" Ruth looked sharply at me.

For a second, I had no idea what she was thinking, but slowly her idea became clear. The family in the woods. I shook my head, hoping no one could see my heart thudding against my ribcage. Telling our parents about the family was one thing, but involving the whole youth group would only multiply the problem and put Patch in even more danger.

"What, Ruth?" Doug asked.

I grabbed her arm and held tight. *Don't say it, Ruth. Don't.*

She tossed me an exasperated look before she said, "Well, maybe we could find some people in our own community who need help. We could get presents for them."

"Oh, and a tree!" Bea said. "We could bring a decorated tree, and presents and Christmas Eve dinner ... to someone who wouldn't have any of those things otherwise."

"Everyone has a Christmas tree." Ted rolled his eyes.

"You'd be surprised," Penny said from her windowseat perch. "I think we've got the beginning of a fantastic idea here."

"Let's break into teams," Doug said, "First, brainstorm what we'll need to pull this off. If you want to work on presents, meet over there." He pointed to the pillows by a windowseat. "Decorations by the books. Food by the snack table, and research up here with me. No need to do anything yet. Just break the project into manageable steps."

"Don't you see?" Ruth asked as soon as people started to move. "Sadie, this is the perfect answer. You didn't know how to convince the girl to listen to you ... this is it."

"Ruth, if the entire youth group hikes out to the shack, they'll disturb Patch. And Christmas is weeks away, too, so how will giving gifts to the family make any difference? The problem is now. The little girl could tell about Patch any second."

"But she hasn't told yet. Sadie, they live in the freezing cold. Obviously they need help."

"Sadie, Ruth, you guys okay?" Doug asked.

"Yes. We're fine." I steered Ruth over to the decoration group, where she ignored me as the group brainstormed ornaments to make on a tight budget.

After about ten minutes, Doug called, "Come on back."

He gathered feedback from all the groups.

"So, sounds like Penny will head up the tree-cutting expedition, which we'll do December twenty third. The decoration committee will create glass ornaments that will catch the lights — thank you, Sadie — and the presents committee is going to shovel snow — thank you Cameron — as a fundraiser so we can purchase gifts. The research committee will ask Pastor George if he knows of a family in need."

Ruth shot me a look, and I shook my head, whispering quietly, "After we talk to the girl, we'll decide what to do. Okay?"

Doug continued. "The food committee will bake on Christmas Eve, and we'll gather that night to deliver the celebration, complete with caroling and hot chocolate."

"And we'll have pizza before we go," Ted said.

"Right. How could I forget the pizza?" Doug asked.

From: Sadie Douglas
To: Pippa Reynolds
Date: Thursday, December 2, 10:05 PM
Subject: Mom

Mom was sick again tonight. I guess I should be grateful that she had so many good days in a row, but I can't be grateful, Pips. Dad found a new treatment online, and he asked me if I thought he should show it to Mom. How am I supposed to know? I guess he should, if he's sure it will work. But no one wants her to go through a whole new round of hospital visits and exhausting treatments that only disappoint us in the end.

Chapter 12

Fused Glass

On the way to the town library the next day, I fingered the small compass in my pocket, which I had found instead of a map piece in drawer three.

"Just open all the drawers already!" Ruth said as we pulled off our scarves and mittens and hung them to dry. "You're driving me crazy!"

The librarian had left our piles of books on our tables.

Ruth sat, took the first book off her pile and sighed. "I will never finish."

"Don't do everything. If Mario doesn't help, Ms. Barton will see that you did your part."

Tess and Nicole's raised voices carried across the library. "Just because you have diamond earrings, you're suddenly better than us?" Tess asked Frankie. Was she being loud on purpose?

"Give me my backpack," Frankie said, her voice low and demanding.

"Even if you move to New York," Nicole said, equally loudly, "Owl Creek will always be your home. It's in your blood."

Frankie shoved Nicole so hard that she stumbled back and fell onto a bench. The backpack tumbled out of her arms and clattered onto the floor.

"Frankie!" Ms. Barton said. "Come with me."

Ms. Barton took Frankie into one of the study rooms and closed the door. Tess and Nicole took their books to Ty's table, where all three leaned their heads together and whispered.

Through the study room windows, I watched Frankie sit stone faced as Ms. Barton spoke to her. I couldn't put the pieces together—the haircut, the pierced ears, Frankie's anger. Did Frankie's mom live in New York? If so, why was Frankie so unwilling to talk about it?

"What if the family in the woods is Jewish?" Ruth looked up from her book on Jewish history. "We can't bring them a tree if they celebrate Hanukkah."

"Ruth, until we go out there—"

"Go out where?" Frankie asked, sliding onto the bench across from us.

I jumped in my seat. Neither Ruth nor I had seen her come back from Ms. Barton.

"Sheesh Frankie, you scared me!" I said. Ruth wordlessly went back to reading her book.

I handed my book to Frankie. "Take a look at this one—there's a lot on food."

"What is it, some big secret?" Frankie asked.

Ruth caught my eye. Perfect. The only thing worse than the youth group knowing about the family in the woods was Frankie knowing, or more specifically, Frankie's dad. The girl knew about Patch's den, and I meant to keep Patch far away from Jim Paulson.

"Ruth and I are making ornaments for a tree that our youth group is giving as a Christmas present. You know, to a family who wouldn't have one otherwise."

"So where are you going?" Frankie leaned forward, her interest no longer casual.

I racked my mind for the dullest possible answer. "To collect glass bottles. We're going to break glass to make into ornaments."

Frankie closed her book and gave me the look she had given me that first day I met her in Moose Tracks Trading Post, her narrowed eyes full of warning. Obviously, I was avoiding her question, but something larger seemed to be bothering her too, as though Frankie had a secret of her own.

"How will you make broken glass into ornaments?" she asked lightly, testing me.

"Vivian uses shards of glass all the time. She presses them into clay or cement and lets it harden. So there's no sharp edges, but the glass still catches the light. I watched her do it. Back when I was taking lessons with her."

"Clay will be too heavy for a tree. You should do fused glass instead." Frankie watched my reaction to this, as though she still didn't believe we'd been talking about ornaments in the first place.

Fused glass? What did Frankie know about fused glass? We all worked in silence for a few moments, and my heartbeat slowed, settling back into a normal rhythm.

"Can I help?" Frankie asked. "With the ornaments?"

The question—so direct, so sudden, so totally unexpected—was like a punch in the stomach. She hadn't looked up from her book. Was this another test? Frankie wanted to know if I knew her secret, whatever it was. Still her voice was entirely without the usual bite. And she did know about fused glass, whatever that was. Maybe she actually wanted to help.

"Ummm ..." I said. "I guess so. Maybe."

Ruth kicked me under the table. I kicked her back. What did she expect me to do? Frankie was somehow, weirdly, trying to be our friend.

Frankie looked up at me then, smiled her sad half-smile. "Thanks, Sadie."

Either I was totally mistaken, or she really meant it.

From: Sadie Douglas
To: Pippa Reynolds
Date: Friday, December 3, 8:45 PM
Subject: Re: Cocoa in the dog house

Poor Cocoa. He can't help eating the mini-quiches when they sit out cooling on the counter, tempting him. Higgins would do the same. I can just see your mom coming downstairs for the party, all freshened up, and finding the trail of crumbs. I still think he should get a doggie stocking for Christmas. He's good most of the time.

Your book idea is working! I have been copying drawings from this book of crazy pictures that look like two things at once. But of course, my copies don't look as good as the originals, which is a little depressing. Still, I'm trying, and I think I'm learning.

Dad said he'd drive me out to the research cabin tomorrow, after we decorate a little with Mom. He has to pick up something from Helen. That's good and bad, because it means I won't be able to hike out to the shack tomorrow because it will be too late, but at least I might be able to set something up with Andrew for Sunday. I hope so. I still haven't heard any bad news about Patch, so I'm starting to hope. Maybe the family in the woods won't find her after all.

Mom is feeling better, I think. She slept all day. I don't think Dad talked to her about the new treatment yet.

Chapter 13

Garland

"Grab this box, Sades." Dad handed me yet another overstuffed box from the attic.

Mid-ladder I paused, my arms aching from the million other boxes I had already lifted down. Mom sifted through a sea of boxes and paper, oohing and ahhing over a camel here, a Santa there. Higgins, wisely, watched from downstairs. But Christmas wouldn't be the same without all of this production. The best part was Mom's smile, her sparkly eyes. Sometimes, when the exhaustion came, she shrunk deep into herself, and her eyes became like a dark cave opening. No matter how deep I looked, I couldn't see Mom. Days like today when she expanded back into herself made me feel more my right size, too. Mom was here, doing all the Mom things, so I could be Sadie, doing all the Sadie things. I'd decorate the house every day if it meant she could be here with us, really here.

"We're missing a bunch of trees, Matthew," Mom said. "Are there some black plastic bags up there?"

Dad poked his dusty head out and grinned at her. "One never-ending flock of plastic-bag-covered trees coming right up."

Mom held the world record for number of Christmas trees displayed in one house — all fake, except for our one, official Christmas tree. I had fought, year after year, for a real, pine-smelling tree from the forest. Even though pine needles made my nose run and my eyes water, I refused to give up any part of the tree-cutting tradition, Dad and I choosing the perfect tree, taking turns sawing, wrapping the branches in rope, lifting the bundle onto the Jeep, driving home and stringing the lights, and then finding the exact right branch for each mismatched, memory-filled ornament.

Dad handed down bags of trees of every size protected by black mylar. We passed them to Mom until I thought we might be buried alive. Policemen would come to the house and poke around, speculating.

"What happened to them, Jones?"

"Not sure, Davis. Appears they were suffocated by Christmas spirit."

Mom interrupted my exhaustion-induced daydream. "Matthew, we're still missing one. The tall, skinny one. I want to put it on the landing with all the boat ornaments."

The ceiling creaked and groaned as Dad crawled deep into the attic.

He dragged out yet another tree. "Stand on the ground for this one, Sades. It's heavy."

After I set the bag down, I collapsed onto the pile of bags. "Enough. Time for cookies."

Mom and I had spent the morning making our favorite Christmas cookies, red and white almond flavored dough twisted together into candy cane shapes. I had wrapped a ziplock bag full of peppermints in a towel and crushed the candy with a rubber mallet on the sunroom floor. We'd sprinkled the minty powder on top of the cookies, fresh out of the oven, so the sugar melted just enough to stick.

I brought up a plate of cookies from the kitchen, and we sat on the stairs while Mom gave us our marching orders. First, distribute the trees around the house. Wrap white fluff around their metal bases to give the illusion of snow. As if anyone needed more snow than the foot-deep snowbanks outside. Next, match boxes of ornaments to the correct tree. Some trees only had lights, but most had themes. Santas, boats, trains...

"Sadie, are you listening?" Mom asked.

"What?" Every last cookie on the plate had disappeared. "Who ate all the cookies?"

"After the ornaments, you're in charge of the garland."

I grinned. "Yep! Ready when you are!"

I took the plate downstairs, put in a Christmas CD, and got to work. After four hours of decorating, every surface, corner, and wall glittered with Christmas cheer. We packed up the empty boxes and lifted them back into the attic.

"Ready to go to the cabin, Sades?" Dad asked.

Finally. I stuffed my feet into my boots, put on my coat, and hurried out to the Jeep.

Dad pulled the Jeep out of our driveway, and snow crunched under its tires. "What did the Advent calendar bring today?"

"Another map piece. So far I've gotten three sections of the map and a compass."

"A compass? So this is a true adventure, it seems."

"Come on, Dad. Admit you made the calendar."

"Can't say that I did."

Even though our speed topped out at fifteen miles an hour all the way to the cabin, Dad made screeching sounds as we rounded corners, trying to be funny. I turned up the radio, but he simply screeched louder. No matter how worried I became, Dad could always make me smile.

Snow flew up behind us as Dad pulled into the research cabin's long driveway. "Here we are." He opened my door and helped me down.

Dad knocked, and we heard a faint, "Come in!"

Dad threw open the front door, stomping off his boots in the mudroom and blowing on his freezing fingers. We hung up our coats and went through the inner door. Helen was stirring a pot on the stove, and cinnamon-apple steam wafted our way. Andrew was sitting in the living room with a textbook and a notebook. Sometimes he pretended to do math or English, but mostly, he just helped his mom and called it homeschool.

"Hallelujah! You saved me from the quadratic equation." He leapt off the couch.

I hadn't expected such an enthusiastic greeting. In fact, I hadn't expected a greeting at all. I sat on a kitchen stool and watched Andrew, trying to decide how to bring up a hike to the shack.

Helen poured Dad and me mugs of cider. I blew on the steam and followed Helen to the file-covered kitchen table.

"I've gathered enough data on the behavior of black bears in this area," Helen began. "I already told you my first research idea, to identify nursing sows that will take an orphaned cub into their dens. DNR agents spend hundreds of hours rehabilitating and relocating orphaned cubs. They want to radio collar trusted bears in the summer and watch over their dens in the winter."

I picked up a file, so dense with text I couldn't possibly skim it and gather any information. Andrew sat next to me, so I pretended to browse the file anyway.

"What's the other idea?" I asked Helen.

"Another scientist has findings that match mine, that bluff charges aren't aggressive acts. Right now, bears can be labeled category two and removed from their habitat if they huff and blow and stomp their front paws. But my findings show that behavior is just bluster. The bears just want to be left alone, and are trying to scare intruders enough so they'll leave."

Dad flipped through one file after another. "How can I help?"

"Meredith wants you to give both questions an unbiased look. She knows I feel strongly about both of these issues and wants me to run my research by you before I write a proposal."

I felt Andrew's eyes on me as I sipped my cider again. Even though he had uninvited me to his house and had acted like I ruined Thanksgiving, I had to talk to him. Patch was in danger.

"I wonder," I said, compromising with a half-look at Andrew, "if we could hike back out past Patch's den. I mean, we know the family in the woods isn't dangerous or anything."

"Are you kids willing?" Helen swept her hand over the folders piled on the table. "I can't find time to hike out there, and I worry about Patch."

Finally — a bit of good luck. "Sure."

"I'd like that," Andrew said.

He'd like that? I couldn't keep up with Andrew these days. Was he angry with me or not? Was I angry with him?

"Ruth said she'd like to come, too," I added.

"Oh, yeah. Okay," Andrew said.

Helen gathered the files into a box. "I know it's a lot, Matthew. You don't have to read it all. Just see if there's reasonable cause for more research."

I took a last sip of my cider and washed my cup. "Thanks for the cider, Helen."

"Sadie." Andrew caught my elbow. "So, you'll come tomorrow then? You and Ruth, I mean."

I looked at Andrew's face for the first time since I had walked in that day. His expression took me completely by surprise. He hurried back to his homework on the couch, but not before I saw his unspoken question. *Are we okay?*

For some reason that I totally didn't understand, Andrew was nervous.

From: Sadie Douglas
To: Pippa Reynolds
Date: Saturday, December 4, 8:45 PM
Subject: The perfect present for Mom

While we stuffed trees into every possible corner in the house, I realized what Mom needs is a new tree! No, really, Pips. A bear tree. What do you think? Moose Tracks has a whole selection of bear ornaments for a dollar or two each.

How's Cocoa? Did you get his picture taken with Santa? Don't forget to bring lots of treats. Remember what happened to the tree display last year? I don't think they do Santa pictures at the pet store here, but I'll check.

Dad and I cut down the Christmas tree tonight, by flashlight, and brought it home. I've got the lights on, and tomorrow I'm putting up all the ornaments.

Wear the blue dress to the holiday party, the one that matches your eyes. And send pictures.

Chapter 14

Shotgun

Sunday afternoon was bitter cold, much too cold for snow to fall. An icy shell had formed over the snow. Helen waved us off as we snow-shoed away from the research cabin. She needed to finish writing a grant proposal.

Along the way, neither Ruth, Andrew, nor I spoke. Our scarves were wrapped around our faces so air made contact with the least possible amount of skin. Still, I wished I had worn my ski goggles, making my protective layer complete.

Andrew glanced my way every once in a while, still wearing the odd expression from yesterday. I wished he wouldn't. Ever since that look first crossed his face, a little winged being had moved into the area around my heart, flitting and fluttering and fanning to life the hope about Andrew and the advent calendar. The map grew, piece by piece, every morning, and I couldn't help wondering what I would find at the end of the search. *Stop it, Sadie. Just stop.*

I hardly paid attention to the passing forest as we wove through pine trees, across the wind-swept meadow, and finally slipped back into the shelter of the trees. Soon, the cabin would emerge from the trees. What then? Would we tramp up to the front door and peek in the window?

"Wait." I reached for the others, realizing I was breathless from cold. "We need a plan. I want to talk to the little girl without her parents."

Ruth shivered and rubbed her jacket sleeves. "We could invite her to go for a hike with us? Like we want to make friends, now that everyone knows about one another?"

I looked at Andrew. "Would that be strange? She's so much younger than us."

"We can try," Andrew said. "At least we'll have an excuse to knock on the door. We should make some noise, too, so we don't startle them."

We started laughing and joking as we hiked, and when the cabin came into sight, Ruth shouted, "We're here!"

Other than the smoke coming from the chimney, the shack showed no other signs of life as we walked up to the door. Andrew knocked and no one answered. After waiting all week, I couldn't stand to go home with no answers. The story about someone buying the shack for this family didn't match up with the little girl's fear. No matter how much Helen or Dad told me not to worry, I couldn't help it. I motioned to the doorknob, silently asking if we should try the door.

Ruth shook her head violently. "What if they're in there?"

Andrew whispered, "Then we'll give them fair warning." He knocked again and said loudly, "That's funny. Smoke is rising from the chimney. Maybe I should open the door and take a look. Wouldn't want the cabin to burn down …"

His words had the desired effect. The door creaked slowly open, and the little girl's green eyes locked with mine.

"What are you doing here?" she demanded. "Mom and Dad will be home any second."

"We came to talk to you." I tried to look past her into the shack.

The girl pushed the door closed. "This is our house and no one can take it from us."

Andrew blocked the door from closing with his foot. "We hiked a long way to see you."

I gave Andrew a warning look. The girl was young, and I could see we were scaring her. "I'm sorry we sent our parents out here to check on you, but we were worried. This shack isn't a proper house for a family. We just thought—"

The little girl frowned and looked behind her. "Nothing's wrong with our house."

Andrew took the opportunity to push the door open enough so we could see inside. "Why don't you let us see, then?"

I scanned the room and understood what Dad had meant about the fixed-up shack. A crackling fire in a wood stove filled the room with warmth and lit up the cozy jumble of furniture—a corduroy couch, a quilt-topped bed, a round table with four chairs that someone had topped with a vase of pine sprigs. A cabinet on wheels that looked like it had once served as a kitchen island leaned against a wall next to an industrial-size water dispenser. The little girl watched us take in the room. The baby was sleeping in a car seat next to the fire. Diapers hung above the fireplace. Even though the furniture looked like it belonged in a garage sale, the little room looked cared for. A smell of orange cleaner mixed with wood smoke and pine.

"But this isn't a home." Ruth looked as confused as I felt. "And you shouldn't be alone here with a baby."

"Our house is perfect. And when my parents find the bear—" The little girl covered her mouth.

I glanced at Andrew and then said to the little girl, "You didn't tell them about the bear?"

The little girl glared at me, but didn't say anything. I thought back to our conversation in the woods. Maybe she had only heard us talking about Patch, and that was what she had meant by her threat. I hadn't heard the rustling until we were at least half a mile from the den. If her parents were still looking for the bear, Patch was safe for now. And I wasn't even sure I could find the den if I didn't know exactly what to look for, so maybe the girl's parents wouldn't find Patch. I could hope anyway.

The baby fussed and the girl picked her up. "My parents will be home any second."

"If they find the bear, what will happen?" Andrew asked.

"It's a treasure hunt," the little girl said, as though these exact words had been used to explain the situation to her.

"If we find the bear, we can live here, together, forever and ever."

"Who told you—" Andrew's question stopped as voices neared, not close enough for us to be seen yet, but too close for comfort.

Ruth, Andrew, and I caught one another's eyes and made an instant decision. We bolted toward the bushes furthest from the voices, fighting our snowshoes as we climbed the hillside and dove behind an outhouse. Seconds later, the little girl's parents hiked down the opposite snowbank to the cabin. Fortunately, they were too deep in conversation to notice our tracks.

"Do you really think that was a bear den?" The woman pulled off her hat and shook snow out of her long hair. "Not just another dark hole in the snow?"

"I'll go back with my shotgun later," the man said. "I didn't want to move any closer without protection. He said the bear was dangerous."

The door closed behind them, and Andrew, Ruth, and I stood for a moment, silent.

"They might not have found her," Ruth said.

"I have to go look for tracks." Andrew stood up and tightened his snowshoes.

I caught the back of his jacket. "But what if we just lead them to her?"

"If he's headed to Patch's den with a shotgun, Sadie, I want to be there to meet him. He can't shoot a hibernating bear if there are witnesses. The DNR would be all over him."

"Maybe they didn't find her," Ruth said again. "We'll hide our tracks the best we can, but I agree with Andrew. We have to know."

I followed, my hands fluttering like birds that couldn't find a place to rest. Every time I caught them and tried to hold them together, they launched into motion again with minds of their own. *Please, let Patch be safe.*

We took a wide, rambling path to the den, using pine branches to muss the snow both where we had walked and also where we had not walked. Finally, we came to Patch's hillside, and we scanned the snow for tracks. Nothing.

"Stay here." Andrew cut a wide circle around the hillside, looking for footprints, checking for broken branches or leaves swept clean of snow.

He finally walked back, shaking his head. "No one has been here."

"Let's make a mess," Ruth said. "We'll track up the snow and totally confuse them."

Andrew and I nodded and we all took off, leaving trails leading to nowhere in every direction, mussing our prints so it appeared we had been trying to cover our tracks. Finally, after about an hour, we turned back for home.

The hike back was long and even colder than the hike out to the shack. None of us said much until we reached the bushes that edged the research cabin's property line.

Andrew, who was a few yards ahead, stopped and turned back to us.

"You want to look at glass for ornaments, right? Let's go talk in the garage."

One bare lightbulb hung from the ceiling in the research cabin's garage, casting dim light over a jumble of boxes and bins. Andrew led me and Ruth past stacks of empty bins to cardboard boxes filled with glass bottles and jars. Since the cabin had no recycling service, Helen and Andrew saved bottles until they had a truckload of them and then took them into town.

Andrew unwound his scarf and took off his gloves so he could rub his red cheeks. "I don't know how you're going to make these ornaments. But we have plenty of glass."

I opened a box full of green, brownish red, clear, and even a few blue bottles. "Perfect."

"Who would have promised that family the shack if they find the bear?" Andrew asked.

"The land company?" Ruth blew into her hands. "That doesn't make sense."

"Could it be Jim?" I sat down on a box. Everything was impossible and so terribly wrong. The little girl, hopeful and desperate, believing an old shack could be a home. Patch, in danger of being shot in her den. Jim, sure Patch was dangerous, willing to go to huge lengths to kill her.

"Maybe," Andrew said. "But no one has found Patch yet, and that's a good sign. Maybe we just wait it out. Soon the big snowstorms will come, and it will be even harder to find the den."

"Oh! Frankie," Ruth said. "Maybe we can get answers from her. You think she knows?"

Andrew flipped around to stare at us. "Frankie?"

"She's back. And something weird is up with her." Ruth sat down on the box next to me. "Her friends are all mad at her, and she keeps hanging out with us."

"Because she's trying to find Patch?" Andrew asked.

Andrew's question made anger rush to my cheeks unexpectedly. "Frankie and her dad are not the same person. Maybe she just ..."

"Just what?" Andrew asked, when I didn't finish my sentence.

I couldn't look at him. "Maybe she just needs a friend."

From: Sadie Douglas
To: Pippa Reynolds
Date: Sunday, December 5, 7:32 PM
Subject: A Match!

Two of my map pieces matched today! I have no idea how you pulled this amazing present off. And stop pretending you didn't give it to me. I know it has to be from you. I just can't figure out how you made bells ring that first morning. But I know you'll tell me when I call you on Christmas. WHAT am I going to give you?

From: Sadie Douglas
To: Pippa Reynolds
Date: Monday, December 6, 5:44 PM
Subject: Frankie

Every day, she seems more and more like a real friend. Like today, she whispered jokes to me under her breath in class, like she used to do with Tess and Nicole. What does it mean?

From: Sadie Douglas
To: Pippa Reynolds, Juliet Chance, Alice Cheng, Brianna Ingles
Date: Tuesday, December 7, 8:13 PM
Subject: Even though I'm not there, you have to promise to . . .

1. Ice skate on the outdoor rink in San Jose.
2. Visit the festival of trees and vote on the best tree of the year.
3. Wear Santa hats to school on the Friday before Christmas break.
4. Promise to send me pictures! I miss you all!

From: Sadie Douglas
To: Pippa Reynolds
Date: Wednesday, December 8, 7:17 PM
Subject: Re: Present for Ryan

I like the idea of the pizza-sized decorated gingerbread cookie. Ryan will love it, I'm sure. I can't decide if I should buy anything for Andrew at all. He's acting so weird. Tonight, he called to ask if he could come to youth group with us tomorrow. I think he doesn't trust me. He keeps telling me that we shouldn't tell the youth group about the family in the woods (Ruth told him her idea on Sunday), and I keep telling him I don't plan to tell, but if he's really worried, he should talk to Ruth, because there's no telling what she'll do. And he snaps my head off every time I bring up Frankie. If he's so mad at me, why does he bother to call?

Chapter 15

Listening is Love

"We've talked a lot about noticing God in our everyday lives." Doug rubbed his hands together then leaned forward, hands on knees. I had seen him do this enough to know that he was truly excited about whatever would come next.

Andrew sat between Ruth and me. Tension stretched tight between the three of us. We avoided the touchy subjects, not mentioning the family in the woods, Frankie, or Patch.

Doug continued, "So now I think we're ready to push our conversation deeper. To challenge ourselves. It's perfect timing really, in this season when gift giving is so important. What does God want to give us? What ought we give to God?"

Claudia's hand shot up. "Pure hearts. God wants us to not sin."

I folded my fingers together in my lap and stared down at my hands. Perfect. On the first night Andrew shows up, Claudia brings up sin. The word sounded so simple and clean-edged slipping from Claudia's mouth, like a perfectly packed moving box taped tightly shut. Sin, a category completely defined by this word. Either something fit inside the sin box or it didn't.

No one spoke for a long moment. Ruth squirmed next to me. I knew she wanted to say something, and also that she would choose walking barefoot in the snow on a minus ten degree day over saying something. No one liked to take Claudia on, because Claudia felt comfortable with thick brush stroke answers. Grey areas confused her, made her lash out. Claudia wanted clear definition. What was right? What was wrong? I didn't blame her, really. Life would be a lot simpler if there were some easy formula. I had no idea what would be in a sin box if I tried to categorize, and I preferred Claudia's tightly taped box to my own, with odd-shaped items sticking out every which way so the box was impossible to close.

I could almost hear Ruth's inward sigh as she finally cleared her throat. "But we do sin. Everyone sins. If we go around trying not to do something, knowing we'll fail over and over again, thinking God wants us to be this person we can never be, how is that helpful?"

"So we shouldn't even try to be good?" Claudia snapped, predictably.

Doug nodded his head slowly. "This is a good conversation. Claudia, you point out that God desires our pure hearts. Ruth, you remind us that God knows our hearts aren't completely pure, can never be completely pure. If we return to what we know—God shows up in the tiniest of moments, God is with us in joy and sadness, God loves us—we find traces of an answer. God doesn't want us to torture ourselves over our imperfection. Yet, he wants us to do our best too."

"Like football," Ted chimed in, causing everyone to groan. "No really. Even though we know we'll never run the perfect play—the other guys will always be in the way—we practice for perfection. Otherwise, we'd be a team of losers."

Doug laughed. "I never thought of it that way, Ted, but I agree with you. This is why I love talking with you guys. I learn so much. We'll discuss these questions in the upcoming weeks. What does God want to give us? What ought we to give him? Millions of sermons have been written on the subject, and I'm sure tons of answers leap to your minds. But I want you to watch. Notice God in your own lives. Maybe by finding answers in our own lives, we'll be able to make the less tangible answers, such as giving God a pure heart, more real for ourselves."

We broke into our groups, and I finally dared looking up at Andrew. He didn't look too freaked out. I remembered Thanksgiving, how Helen had suggested we pray. I had never talked to Andrew about God, and I had no idea if he believed in anything or not. I always assumed people didn't, maybe because my family didn't, but the more I hung out at youth group the more I wondered. People thought about

God a lot more than I realized. And not just people who went to church. Normal people, even Mom, thought about God, especially when people needed help. If people believed in God when they needed help, then they must believe in him all the time. Maybe they just needed to pay more attention. My mind felt over full. I hugged my legs to my chest.

"Andrew looked up fused glass online with us today," Ruth said to Georgia and Nick, our other two group mates. Georgia and Nick were both Jasper's age, fifth graders, pretty much willing to do whatever we asked. Georgia had long white-blond hair and was almost painfully shy. Nick was constantly fidgeting, doodling with one hand while constantly changing position. "Andrew wants to help with the project."

"Ruth, Sadie, and I will break the glass, and we'll look for someone with a rock tumbler. We have to tumble the glass to make the edges smooth," Andrew said. His hands outlined the glass bottle and the tumbler in the air in front of him, the way he did when he got excited about something.

"Sadie will ask Vivian Harris if we can all come to her studio to shape the ornaments and put them into the kiln. I suppose we should try to make ... how many ornaments do you think?"

"One hundred?" Ruth glanced at the tree group. "Knowing Penny, it will be a big tree."

"It doesn't look like the ornament making process is all that hard," Andrew said. "We have to keep each bottle separate because glass melts at different temperatures, and we have no way to determine the melting point of used glass. So we'll tumble one bottle at a time. I'd bet we could get ten ornaments from one bottle."

Nick looked up from his notebook. "My cousin has a rock tumbler. Want me to get it?"

"Yes!" Andrew actually grabbed both of Nick's hands and shook them up and down.

Why was he so excited about the project? And the conversation sped by so fast, I only barely registered the part about me inviting us all over to Vivian's house. Complication after complication. Still, I hadn't seen Andrew looking so excited for what felt like forever. After the weirdness between us, his smile untied a knot inside me, one I hadn't known was there. Maybe Andrew and I could be friends, and things could be okay. If I went to see Vivian.

Doug knelt down by Andrew. "Well, sir? What do you think of our group?"

"We've got a good plan for the ornaments," Andrew said.

Doug listened carefully as Andrew explained, and then said, "Sounds a little complex, but definitely possible. You're up for the challenge?" He looked around at the group. Everyone else nodded, while I sighed inwardly. "You too, Sadie?" Doug asked.

I caught Andrew's eye. What else could I say? "Yes."

"We found a family, Doug," Ruth said, catching me totally off-guard.

Both Andrew and I lunged for Ruth, but I grabbed her elbow first.

I forced a smile for Doug's sake. "We can tell you about it later. Anyway, doesn't the research group have some ideas?"

"They do, but I'd love to hear your idea, girls. Can you stay after tonight?"

"No. Sorry. It's just that Mom is picking us up tonight and ..." I'd never been so happy to use Mom as an excuse.

"Well, maybe you can give me a call this week, or come out one afternoon after school. It's probably best that we discuss particulars on our own, instead of in front of the group."

"Sure," Ruth said.

I released my grip.

"What are you doing, Ruth?" Andrew asked, looking from me to Ruth to me again.

"Don't you think that if we bring them a tree and presents, they will have to listen to us? We'll just explain to them about Jim and ..."

Anger flashed across Andrew's face, but I held out my arm to stop him from yelling, realizing I was standing between the two of them, blocking them from one another.

"Promise you won't tell Doug or anyone else until we all agree," I said. "Please, Ruth."

She looked into my eyes and then over my shoulder at Andrew. "I can't. I can't ignore them. There's a baby living in a shack in the forest. They need help."

I watched her walk out the door, felt Andrew's muscles tense, felt the space between all of us widen. Once, Ruth had made me a promise she couldn't keep and then broken it, almost breaking our friendship in the process. So in a way, not promising was the right thing to do, the true friend thing to do. Still, Ruth's honesty didn't make her non-promise any easier.

I turned to Andrew. "I'll talk to her." I didn't add, *It will be fine,* because like Ruth, I needed to stop lying and start being a true friend, even when the truth hurt.

From: Sadie Douglas
To: Pippa Reynolds
Date: Thursday, December 9, 9:56 PM
Subject: Andrew

Andrew is still acting weird. Tonight, he apologized for thinking I wanted to tell about the family in the woods. But then he shuffled his feet and wouldn't look me in the eyes. He's been strange ever since Thanksgiving. I don't like this.

Chapter 16

Words and Pictures

Pieces of the map now piled up on my desk. Each origami figure had pulled open to reveal yet another three inch square section. In the early morning light, I moved the pieces around, matching one end to another. Three pieces of a path or a road matched from one piece to another, but I wasn't sure about the rest.

A white star had been painted onto drawer ten. I pulled it open and took out the origami bird inside. None of the other origami shapes had been as intricate as this, and as with the first star, I really didn't want to pull it open. I took the bird to the bathroom and let her watch me brush my teeth and wash my face.

"You ready to do this thing?" I asked her after I'd done every last get-ready task.

I pulled her tail up and away, and smoothed the paper

open. This time, there was no map. Instead, the paper held scrawled instructions. *Go to your favorite place, high above the snow. Look with far-reaching eyes, and you'll find what you need.*

A treasure hunt. I really wanted to go right now, but since I had to face Vivian today, I decided to save the clue for afterward. A needed reward.

After school, Dad drove me to Vivian's house. "I can't wait for more than half an hour, Sades. I need to get back to work."

"Okay. I don't think this will take long."

"You're sure she's here?"

No. But I hadn't been able to bring myself to call ahead. "I'll hurry."

Snow fell in huge flakes today, frosting my eyebrows and running tear-like down my cheeks. No one had bothered to clear the snow from Vivian's front steps, which made sense, since Peter had left town after the trial. I hesitated in front of the door, the echoes of Peter and Vivian and my laughter over drawings and hot cocoa and stories loud in my ears. I didn't want to go inside, didn't want to see how different everything was now.

Still, I forced myself to ring the doorbell. Almost immediately, her footsteps sounded down the front hall, the quick, purposeful rhythm I had learned to listen for unconsciously as I sat at the drawing table. Vivian always knew exactly how long to let me draw. Just when I began to doubt the shapes on my page, I heard those footsteps. Vivian would bustle in with a steaming cup of tea or a plate of fresh strawberries and ask a question that first made me want to throw my pencils against the wall. But then, as I struggled to find an answer, the fog would lift, and I would see the next few steps of my way clearly. Everything had been fog since I'd last been to Vivian's house. At least as far as drawing was concerned. Maybe as far as everything was concerned. But you couldn't spend your life counting on someone else to lift your fog, particularly when that person might let you down in the end.

Even though I wasn't ready, would never be ready, the door opened.

Vivian wore her red apron, splattered with dried paint and dusted with flour, over her usual uniform, jeans and a long sleeve shirt, with her green and yellow polka-dotted socks. The sweet smell of peanut butter cookies baking spilled out onto the snow. Words caught in my throat. Vivian still baked. She still wore polka-dotted socks. She was still Vivian, even though so much had changed.

"Sadie," she said, not quite covering the surprise in her voice. "Is your dad waiting in the Jeep? He can come in." She grabbed her coat. "Here, you come inside and I'll go ..."

"No." The word burst out of me, too loud.

She stopped, as though my shout had paralyzed her.

"I'm sorry," I said. "I just have something quick to ask you. He doesn't mind waiting."

She frowned out toward the Jeep. Then, she nodded and hung the coat back on the hook. "Come in out of the cold, then, Sadie. No need for us to freeze while we talk."

Either Vivian didn't believe in decorating for Christmas, or she hadn't gotten around to it yet. Everything was as I remembered. The floor-to-ceiling fish tank divided the hall from the living room, the orange and blue fish polka dots against the red wall on the other side of the tank.

"You have perfect timing. The cookies are almost done." Vivian led me down the hall into the kitchen.

I sat at the tall counter as she took the baking trays out of the oven.

"I've thought about you often, Sadie," Vivian continued, when I didn't speak. "How is the drawing?"

If only I could swallow the lump in my throat, I could ask about the kiln and leave.

Vivian worked a spatula under each cookie and set them on a baking rack to cool. She put the last two on plates. "One for you and one for me."

I took the plate she held out and stared at the cookie, which swum under my suddenly watery eyes. No. I would not cry.

"There's a lot to say." Vivian said. "You sure we shouldn't invite your dad inside?"

A tear rolled down my cheek before I could stop it. "No. I need to go. I just ..."

"Wait here." Vivian left the plate and walked down the hall to her art studio.

I swiped angrily at my eyes. Here, with Vivian handing me cookies, looking so ordinary in her red apron, I could almost forget how strange everything had become between us. I wanted to go back, back before I'd found out about Peter. Back to when Vivian's house had been my one escape from the mess of the rest of my life.

Vivian returned with a black spiral bound notebook and sat on the stool next to me.

"After the trial, my sketchbook started to change," she said. "At first I didn't want to draw at all. I kept seeing the eyes you drew in your sketchbook, your dad's eyes, over and over. I didn't want to draw for practice, and I didn't want to plan new pieces. I wanted to draw Peter. I wanted to draw him until I didn't only see what I wanted to see, but until I really saw him."

She opened her sketchbook and turned page after page. "I used photos from when he was a little boy, wrote about what I remembered."

Sketchy drawings intermixed with pages of writing, some pages watercolored in intense Vivian colors — mandarin orange, aquamarine, with Peter, mud-streaked and grinning, Peter pouting into an almost empty Halloween bucket, Peter, eyes wide, opening a Christmas present.

"When I built up my courage, I started drawing him as he is now." She turned the page, showing adult Peter at the breakfast table, head in hands. Adult Peter, ax over his shoulder, heading out to cut firewood. Adult Peter looking out the window, a desperate look on his face.

I knew Vivian was trying to tell me something, saying something without saying it. I couldn't say what I needed to say either. How could I put into words how disappointed I had been, all the reasons things would never be the same as they had been?

I swallowed hard. "I haven't been drawing much. I've been trying..."

Without understanding why, I took out my own sketchbook. Talking to Vivian in pictures was simpler than finding the right words. I flipped through my *Starry Night* pictures, through my magical realism pictures, all the false starts for Pips's present.

"Who is this artist you're copying?" Vivian turned page after page. "Such intriguing perspective. I can see why you like her work."

"His name is Ron Gonsalves. You'd think, with his pictures to copy, my pictures wouldn't come out so all wrong."

"How are they wrong?" Vivian asked.

"The perspective. The colors. The light. Sometimes even the shapes are wrong."

"First of all, you're asking something very complex of yourself, Sadie. Perspective is distorted in these images. Perspective, even when it is true to life, is difficult. But also, you're trying so hard to get it right. Your lines are very tight and controlled here. Copying other artists is a fantastic way to learn, to push your skills, but don't forget, skill with a pencil isn't the only important thing. In our last session, you had started to think about the artist's first essential question. Did you ever figure out what it was?"

I thought back to the day I'd run out of Vivian's art studio, too upset to finish my lesson after discovering the truth about Peter. That day, we'd looked at Van Gogh's *Starry Night* and a few other paintings. Up to that point, Vivian had encouraged me to draw only what I saw, and the unrealistic paintings contradicted everything I had learned. I stared down at Vivian's sketchbook. Each image, though different, had a Vivian quality. Her thick strokes faded at the edges, loosely drawn, not painstaking like some of my drawings. All her shapes had a similar rounded-edge feel, and shading played a big part in every scene.

I ran my finger along my sketchbook's spiral spine. "Something about style? The way an artist draws that makes them different, I guess?"

Vivian smiled, and I figured I had at least come close. I also knew she wouldn't ever tell me straight out. She preferred I discover answers myself, and to be honest, I preferred that, too.

I retraced the line of fall trees in my drawing, both treetops for a lower street and leaves scattered on a higher street. Two things at once. The way I was two things now, a girl who wanted nothing but to leave and who also wanted to hear every last thing Vivian would tell me. A girl who believed that maybe Vivian could lift my fog once more and help me move forward.

"We're making ornaments, for youth group. We want to make them out of glass, but we need to fire them in a kiln."

Vivian smiled. "My kiln is at your service."

"There are a lot of us. Ruth, Andrew, and these other two kids, Georgia and Nick. We'd have to come here to lay out the ornaments."

"Yes, the ornaments wouldn't travel well before they are fired. A little party gives me a chance to try a new cookie recipe. Peanut butter has become boring."

My cookie still cooled on my plate. I took a bite, letting the warm, slightly doughy middle melt on my tongue. Leave it to Vivian to make peanut butter cookies in the middle of December, when everyone else busily made Christmas cookies.

"Peanut butter is okay with me."

"I'm here every afternoon next week. Figure out what day works for everyone and let me know. I'll have to fire the kiln once before you come, so give me at least a day's notice. We have to watch the glass carefully when we fire it, so plan to stay for at least four hours after we put the pieces in. Maybe we can order takeout. Sound okay?"

With everyone else here, Vivian and I couldn't get into any deep conversations, so I should be all right.

"Thank you." I finished my cookie and put my sketch-book away.

"Take your dad a cookie." Vivian handed me two cookies on a napkin. "And another for you. For the road."

Chapter 17

Scope

When Dad dropped me off at home, my head was full of Vivian's notebook, which brimmed with messy sketches, scrawled notes, a record of her life from the trial until now, not only daily events, but her thoughts and memories too, all mixed up together, like real life.

After looking at Vivian's notebook my fingers itched to draw, really draw, not just copy art from books. But curiosity could only be held off for so long. I was so impatient to know where the Advent calendar clues led, I didn't bother taking off my coat or boots.

I scratched Higgins's ears and called hello to Mom, who sat with her laptop in her favorite armchair in the living room, and then I hurried up to my room and grabbed the clue, taking my sketchbook too. *My favorite place high above the snow* could only describe one spot. At the end of our second floor hallway, a spiral staircase rose up to a trap door on the ceiling, which opened onto a round porch at the top of our house. I hadn't been up there since the first snowfall.

Pips kept insisting she hadn't made the calendar, and I was starting to wonder. Of course, if it wasn't Pips, it must be Mom and Dad. They loved to do stuff like this. When I'd been younger, my parents used to make an adventure out of my "big" present. They'd wrap a clue in a box under the tree leading to a trail of other clues and ending with the present, something I'd hardly dared to wish for, like my first bicycle.

When I was seven, I secretly wished for my very own theatre, knowing I couldn't have one. Somehow, they'd transformed the downstairs playroom into a stage, complete with a trunk full of costumes and a pipe to hang backgrounds from. Their artist friend painted sheets to look like a castle, a forest, and a candy factory.

A pile of snow fell onto my head when I pushed the trap door open. I shook the snow off my hair and climbed the rest of the way up. Snow had transformed the forest, frosting branches and blanketing the ground.

Look with far-reaching eyes, and you'll find what you need.

I scanned the treetops. Was the clue sending me into the forest? Other than the round railing and the cushioned seat, the porch only held an old telescope, left behind by a former owner of the house. Andrew and I had rolled the telescope over to the railing so we could stargaze, but covered it with canvas when the snow began. I pulled the cover off and squinted through the hole. Nothing. I twisted the dial and looked again. Still nothing. Squinting never worked well for me. I covered my left eye with my hand and yet again, I didn't see anything.

Maybe the snow had broken the telescope. I turned the barrel toward me and brushed snow away. And then I saw it. A folded paper, wedged into the seal that held the lens in place. I pulled it out and unfolded it. Another piece of map, this one with two words: *Turn left*.

Where could my parents be sending me? The map, with trees and paths marked, was obviously not leading to any-place inside our house.

I rotated the telescope so that it pointed back out to the woods and peered through. With my left eye covered, I saw snow-kissed trees in detail through the scope. I uncovered my left eye, focusing hard, trying to see both the detail with my right eye and the distance with my left. Two things at the same time. A tree, individual and particular, and an entire snow-covered forest.

I opened my sketchbook and drew the telescope's outline, making the view finder large enough to show the detailed tree, leaving enough room on the page to sketch in the rest of the forest. As I sketched the tree in the lens-shaped circle, I was tempted to hurry through the branches. But I forced myself to draw these specific branches, this specific tree, the way Vivian had taught me. As I did, I realized the tree tilted at an odd angle, and the snow only tipped branches on one side. Had the wind blown off the rest? Had someone brushed past the tree?

Questions flowed in with each pencil stroke. I hadn't forgotten how to draw, how to look at things. Almost blue with cold, still my fingers flew across my page. I felt like me.

I started scribbling notes beside my drawing, as Vivian had done in her sketchbook. Maybe this wasn't technically the best drawing in the world, but after almost a month of nothing, my fingers finally felt free. I wasn't tensing them, afraid of what might show up on the paper, or trying to perfectly copy from a book. I hadn't realized how much I missed this feeling.

The phone rang and I hurried downstairs to pick it up.

"I'm going to talk to Doug tomorrow," Ruth said. "About the family. Dad is going caroling with a bunch of people, and Doug will be there. I thought I should tell you."

"Ruth—"

"Patch's den is pretty far away from the shack." Ruth pushed on, as though she was reading a rehearsed speech. "And Sadie, those people can't keep living out there in the cold. We have to do something for them."

Finally she gave me room to talk. "I just don't want to do the wrong thing," I said. "I don't want to mess up and hurt Patch. Not after we all fought so hard to keep her safe."

"We can tell Doug about Patch if you want. We can ask him to help us keep her safe, and maybe help the family find a better home."

"I don't think they want to move, Ruth. And Andrew would hate us talking about Patch."

"Andrew thinks everyone is a hunter deep down. He wants

to protect his mom, and they've both seen a lot of bears killed. But Sadie, you know this is the right thing to do."

I wasn't sure it was the right thing to do. But I knew Ruth would tell Doug whether I agreed with her or not. "I'll come with you."

Ruth paused and then asked, "You're sure?"

"Yes, Ruth."

Another long pause where I could hear a muffled conversation with her mom. "Okay. We'll pick you up around six o'clock."

"I'll be ready."

When I hung up, Mom called up. "Sadie, is that trap door open? It's freezing."

"I'll close it!"

I climbed back to the porch to finish my drawing. After looking through the scope once more, I added a few final strokes and then leaned away to examine the page. Done. I closed the book, covered the scope, and closed the trap door on my way inside.

I had finally slipped back inside my own skin.

From: Sadie Douglas
To: Pippa Reynolds
Date: Friday, December 10, 6:07 PM
Subject: Christmas at the DNR

Dad's Christmas party was tonight. Mom wore the red flapper dress that she wore to New Year's at your house. She looked beautiful, Pips, but I couldn't stop thinking about last year, how she collapsed, and we had to take her to the hospital, how that red was so dark against her pale skin. The party was small. Meredith, our family, and a few DNR people. I wish Helen and Andrew could have come. Well maybe. But only if Andrew acted normal.

If your parents are giving Andrea an iPhone, I bet you anything they'll give you one, too. I'm so jealous. Tell the girls hello.

Chapter 18

Angels We Have Heard on High

The sanctuary smelled like lemon wood-polish, perfume, and throat lozenges, so different from the Catholic church downtown, which smelled of wax, dust, and incense. The Catholic church made me want to nestle quietly on a pew or light a candle. This church, with its bright overhead lights and cheerful noise of mingled voices, made me feel I should strike up a conversation with everyone near me. Since I only attended youth group and not regular Sunday service, I rarely came into this sanctuary. But I had been Ruth's friend long enough to meet the church regulars.

Tonight everyone was bundled in coats and scarves, ready to head out to Hiawatha to sing door-to-door. I had never gone caroling or been visited by carolers. "What will they sing?" I asked Ruth.

She pointed to the song books. "They take books out, because most people only know the first verse of Christmas carols."

"I'm not sure I even know the first verses," I said.

"You girls sure you don't want to come?" Ruth's dad asked.

I actually did want to go, but I wasn't sure if that was yet another form of procrastination. I really didn't want to have to talk to Doug about the family in the woods.

Doug appeared through a side door, and as if he read my mind, he said, "May we join you caroling after we meet? If that's okay with you girls, that is."

Ruth looked at me, and I smiled. "I've never been caroling before, but it sounds kind of fun."

Ruth's dad beamed. "I'll bring my cell so you can find us."

The carolers gathered together as Ruth and I followed Doug into his office. Actually it was more like a walk-in closet with three desks and chairs where Penny, Ben, and Doug all worked together. A rat's nest of cables covered Ben's desk. Penny's desk held a wild assortment of random items — hair spray, balloons, glow sticks, and a rubber chicken.

Doug's desk held stacks of papers, organized into piles. He sat on his desk with his foot on his chair. "Have a seat, ladies. Don't mention the rubber chicken. Penny will blow her top if I ruin her surprise."

"What's the chicken for?" I couldn't help asking.

Doug held his hands up in resistance. "I can't tell. I've promised on a double-decker ice cream sundae. As in I will give it up if I spill the beans. So it's not happening."

"Did the research group find a family?" I asked.

"We keep running into dead ends. One suggestion was actually someone from youth group, but the person didn't want everyone to know about his family situation. Which I certainly respect. And a few families in church have deep need, but don't have children. The research group feels strongly that we should choose a family with kids, and I agree."

Ruth nearly bounced in her seat with excitement. "Do you want to tell him, or should I?"

I laced and unlaced my fingers together, again and again. I didn't know which I was more worried about — the danger to Patch or Andrew's anger.

"Sadie, what's wrong?" Doug asked.

Now that we were here, I'd have to tell one way or another, and somehow I had to make Doug understand about Patch. I let out a sigh and began. "Patch is a research bear that almost got killed last hunting season. She finally chose a den a couple miles from the research cabin. We were all relieved because she denned on vacant land."

"It's for sale," Ruth said.

"We've snowshoed out past Patch's den every week or so," I continued, "to make sure no one has found the den. Helen has hiked out there mostly."

"But on Thanksgiving, Sadie, Andrew, and I did the hike," Ruth said. "And we were followed by a little girl."

Ruth pushed her hair behind her ears, getting into the story. "We found out this girl lives with her mom and dad and baby sister in an abandoned cabin in the woods."

"Old Man Mueller's shack," I said.

"I've been out to that shack in the summer," Doug said. "But that's no place for a family in the winter."

I nodded. "Helen, Dad, and Meredith hiked out there and spoke to the family. Someone is buying the land and giving them the shack, which is all fixed up inside. But the story doesn't make sense. And we think they are looking for Patch, for some reason. If they find her ..."

"I can see why you're worried, Sadie." Doug tapped a pen against his leg, thinking.

"Don't you think they are the perfect family, though?" Ruth leaned forward. "I mean, who needs Christmas more than a family in a shack in the middle of the woods?"

"I'll call Helen," Doug said. "Then I'll hike out there with Penny. We'll check it out and go from there."

"But you won't let everyone from youth group go out to the cabin, will you?" I asked. "Patch and her cubs—"

"Her den is far enough away from the shack," Ruth said. "At least a ten minute hike."

Doug set his pen down. "As far as bears go, Sadie's right. Our whole youth group that close to a bear's den could be too much. Someone could wander by the den, or possibly even find it. The noise alone of all those people might cause Patch to come out of her den looking for intruders. Bears shouldn't be roused in the middle of their sleep."

"She wouldn't attack," I said, hoping Doug understood my concerns.

"No, I know that. I've seen Patch eat out of Mrs. Rose's hand. I know Patch," Doug said.

Ruth glanced first at Doug, and then at me, frustration clear on her face. "But how will we bring them Christmas if we don't go out there? It's not enough of an impression if just one or two of us goes. It won't be good enough."

"We'll worry about good enough once we know the particulars. Okay, Ruth?" Doug looked her in the eyes. "I know you want to give a beautiful Christmas to a family." He turned to me. "And I know you do too, Sadie, but I also understand your concerns. We'll figure this out. I promise. Now, what do you girls say we grab a few song books and head out?"

Ruth and I put on gloves, scarves, coats, and hats and climbed into Doug's SUV. The carolers had traveled to west Hiawatha, a neighborhood known for Christmas lights. Doug parked outside the subdivision, and we hiked in, following our ears more than our eyes. Before we could see the crowd, we heard their voices, harmonizing in four parts, singing "Angels We Have Heard on High." Lights sparkled against the snow, lighting up the night, and the acapella music was so rich that as we approached, I could almost imagine angels singing instead of a group from church.

We rounded the corner of a house and saw the carolers standing beside a picket fence, the owners of three or four houses listening from their porches on either side of the street.

"Beautiful, isn't it?" Doug asked.

I nodded, tracing the scene in my mind, memorizing the arcs of light gleaming off the faces of the singers.

"Let's go!" Ruth said.

We ran over and searched through song book pages. When I found the right page, I ran my finger under the words so I wouldn't get lost, all the way up to the Glorias. Then I closed the book, closed my eyes, and let my voice sail up on the slip-stream of music, thick and textured like the waves in Van Gogh's *Starry Night*. In the silence after the song, I opened my eyes.

"You're glowing," Ruth whispered.

I grinned back at her. "So are you."

From: Sadie Douglas
To: Pippa Reynolds
Date: Saturday, December 11, 10:03 PM
Subject: Glass

On our way home from caroling, Ruth called Andrew and asked if we could come to the research cabin tomorrow to break glass. So now I feel bad because I sort of shrugged when Frankie asked if she could help us. That's not a real yes, is it? Because I don't want to have to call her house and ask if she wants to come. Maybe she'll be back at the library tomorrow. I think she's been hanging out there on the weekends because she's in some monster fight with her dad. I'll ask Dad to stop and hope for the best. I don't think things will go too well between her and Andrew if she comes to the research cabin.

Chapter 19

Broken Glass

Dad pulled into the lot behind the library and left the engine running.

"Five minutes, I promise." I walked fast so I couldn't change my mind.

"Morning," the librarian said.

I stomped snow off my boots and unwound my scarf. "Good morning. Is Frankie here?"

"Over there." The librarian nodded toward the back table.

Andrew was going to kill me.

I walked past the stacks to the table. Frankie must have heard me, because she waited, pencil poised above her paper, like she'd paused in the middle of a thought. For a second, I stopped, wanting to draw her just like that, waiting. Frankie never waited. She did things, made things happen.

Now, with her head tilted just slightly, her eyebrows drawn together in the hint of a question, she looked like a painting of herself, done by a painter who didn't really know Frankie, who had caught her in an odd moment and made her into someone she wasn't.

"Want to come to the research cabin?" I asked. "We're breaking glass today."

Frankie grabbed her bag and shoved her stuff inside. "Absolutely."

I rewrapped my scarf as Frankie bundled up. Neither of us spoke on the way to the Jeep. The silence was almost as brittle as the freezing air, until Frankie pulled open the car door.

She climbed in the back. "Hi, Mr. Douglas."

"No one calls me Mr. Douglas in this car. Matthew's just fine, Frankie."

Dad knew Frankie from the community meetings, and of course, he'd heard plenty about her from me. I wondered what he thought of her suddenly appearing now, coming out to the research cabin. I hadn't asked permission, but to be honest, I didn't want permission. In fact, I didn't even want Frankie around. Still, something compelled me to invite her, wouldn't let me avoid inviting her, the way I couldn't have ignored the jingle bells on December first even if I tried. Maybe Doug would say this was God leading me. Certainly, I was as illogical and determined about this as Ruth had been about talking to Doug.

"Sure, okay." Frankie pulled her bag into her lap and hugged it close.

"Frankie is going to help us break glass for the ornaments," I told Dad.

"I still don't understand what these ornaments are going to look like," Dad admitted.

I launched into an explanation of the broken glass, the tumblers, the assembly of shapes such as angels and trees and stars, and the firing in the kiln. I didn't stop to take a breath, didn't stop to let anyone comment. I couldn't. The closer we got to the cabin, the more nervous and talkative I became. Andrew would never understand.

Ruth and Andrew ran out to meet the car, and both stopped as Frankie opened her door.

"Hi," Frankie said.

Andrew opened his mouth, but closed it.

"You kids have fun," Dad said. "I'll be back in two hours unless you call me."

I said goodbye and watched him drive away, and I had to fight the urge to run after him and leave. Instead, I turned back to Andrew and launched back into nervous-talking mode. "Andrew, this is Frankie."

"We've met," he said, his voice almost a growl.

"Right. I knew that, sorry. She wanted to help break the glass. Is everything ready?"

"We were about to grab bags to put the glass into," Ruth said. "From the kitchen."

Frankie fell into step with Ruth, but Andrew caught my arm as they went into the cabin.

"Are you crazy, Sadie?" Andrew asked. "Frankie can't

come out here. You know what her dad will do if they find Patch."

My temper flared hot, probably because I agreed with him. "First of all, I don't know what her dad will do if he finds Patch, and neither do you. And how in the world is being here at the cabin going to help Frankie find Patch? Patch is over an hour away from here."

"I don't know, Sadie. Maybe the bear map in the cabin?"

The map on Helen's study wall, I hadn't even thought about it. It showed the dens of each of the bears.

"She won't go into your mom's study ..."

"My point is, the cabin isn't set up for secrecy, Sadie. We don't need the enemy here."

"I don't know if Frankie is the enemy anymore," I said, getting angry.

"No?" Andrew ran his hands through his hair. "The kind of people who are friends with Frankie aren't the kind of people who are friends with me. You can't be both kinds, Sadie."

"What are you saying?" I asked, my voice a whisper.

Andrew's voice softened, but he didn't sound sorry. He sounded resigned. "It's just the truth."

I would choose Andrew over Frankie any day. Didn't he know that? But anyone, even Andrew, giving me an ultimatum like that made me fighting mad. My fists were so tight that my fingernails dug into my palms.

"Just try to be nice," I said through gritted teeth.

Ruth and Frankie brought a box of garbage bags from the cabin, and we followed them into the garage.

"Double bag each bottle," Ruth said. "Choose the pretty colors. We think we'll be able to make ten ornaments from each bottle, so I guess we should break ten?"

"Maybe twelve to be safe," I said. I chose a green glass bottle.

Andrew didn't say anything as he brought over the hammer. Frankie put her bag in the waiting plastic garbage can, and Andrew started smashing. At first, the can slid all around, particularly since he swung the hammer like an enraged gorilla.

"Let me hold the can for you." Frankie sat down and pinned the can between her knees.

"I'll hurt you," Andrew said, and for a moment, the question hung in my mind — was this a threat or a worry?

"Hit down toward the bottle, and the ground will absorb most of the impact. Just try it." Frankie grabbed the can with her hands too.

Andrew swung and the glass crunched, but the can stayed firm.

Frankie smiled at him.

Andrew shrugged and swung a few more times, more gently than before. Then he handed the hammer to Frankie. "Your turn."

We took turns hitting bottles until all twelve were shards in the bags.

Frankie looked up from the last bottle, out of breath from swinging again and again. "I kind of want to keep going. This is fun."

"Strangely satisfying," Ruth said.

"I know what you mean," Frankie said.

They smiled at each other, a real smile. Maybe this was why I had felt so compelled to bring Frankie over to the cabin. Maybe God wanted ... The thought stopped me short. How was I supposed to know what God wanted? All I knew was right now, Ruth and Frankie together, not just in the same room but breaking glass for the same reason, felt important. And I was proud to be part of it, no matter what Andrew said.

Andrew stayed quiet as we loaded the first bottle into the tumbler and went into the cabin for cookies and hot cocoa. Frankie wandered around the room, looking at the photos. Many of them were bears. Cubs in trees, bears scratching hollow logs for ants, bears facing off with each other, but some pictured Andrew with the bears, or Helen and her favorite bear, Humphrey.

"You aren't scared?" Frankie asked him, standing in front of a picture of Andrew standing in the cabin's front yard with four bears looking up at him. "Look at their claws."

Andrew grunted instead of answering.

"I was scared," I told Frankie. "When I first came to the cabin. Bears roamed the yard, ate from the feeders. I thought one of them would attack me. But I felt less scared the more I watched them."

Shadows moved into her eyes, clouding out the Frankie of the past few hours and reminding me of the other Frankie. Maybe I had pushed too far. Just because we smashed a little glass together didn't mean she'd changed her mind on the bears.

"I don't know," I said. "They're just a lot more peaceful than people think."

"I know you all think I'm wrong and my dad's wrong," Frankie said, folding her arms and facing us like we were a jury to persuade. "But we've lived here a lot longer than any of you. Maybe by letting bears come so close, by feeding them out here, you're making the problem worse. Bears should be afraid of people. They're wild animals, not pets."

"Why did you want to come out here?" Andrew burst out. "To lecture us? What did you think—you'd give your little speech and my mom would go away? I know that's what your dad wants. For us and Sadie's family to all go away and leave you alone."

"I never said ..." Frankie's voice trailed off.

"You said plenty." Andrew turned to me. "Don't bring her out here again, Sadie."

I listened to his footsteps as he went upstairs, down the hall, and into his room. When his door slammed shut, Helen looked out of her office.

"Everything all right?" she asked.

"Yes," Ruth said.

Frankie stared at the floor, and I couldn't have spoken if I had wanted to.

From: Sadie Douglas
To: Pippa Reynolds
Date: Sunday, December 12, 7:15 PM
Subject: Map

So the map is starting to match up, Pips. I can't imagine where
you're sending me. I still don't know what to give you. But don't
worry, I'll come up with something.

Things are a mess. I brought Frankie out to the research cabin
to help us break glass for ornaments, not so much because I
wanted to, but I don't know, because I felt like I had to. There's
something about Frankie right now, like she needs me, and I just
can't ignore that. Andrew got really mad and acted like I had
chosen Frankie over him. It feels like he and I aren't even friends
any more. I can't stand that, Pips, I really can't. If he hates me
now, I mean. And it isn't fair, either. Just because I feel the need
to be nice to Frankie. Why does he have to be so complicated?

I'm sorry about the play. Sleeping Beauty has to get kissed,
though, so maybe it's good you didn't get the part. Only one
more week of school until break. You can make it. Are you giving
Ryan his present on Friday?

Chapter 20

Ribbons and Bows

Monday and Tuesday at school were miserable. Frankie, Ruth, and I tiptoed around conversations that would bring up Andrew, which was difficult. He'd refused to come to the ornament making party at Vivian's. He just dropped off the tumbled glass at her house. During the day, so none of us saw him.

Meanwhile, our presentations were starting on Thursday, and none of us could find any real answers on why our holidays were important.

"People just celebrate because they do," Ruth said on our way to Moose Tracks Trading Post after school. This morning, I'd found another clue in the Advent calendar instead of an actual piece of map. It said: *In the shop of mooses, (or is that meese?) find the gifts that fit in socks. There you'll find what you're looking for.* Ruth and I had convinced our parents to let us go shopping that afternoon. Of course, my parents would have known about the clue, so of course they said yes. Also, this gave us time to do our Christmas shopping, an added bonus.

"Like how Hallmark totally invented Valentine's Day, just to make more money," Ruth continued as we walked into the store.

The familiar smells of coffee and leather wrapped around me.

"But Valentine's Day has become important," I said. "I mean, tell me you'd give it up just because there's no real reason for the holiday."

"No. I guess not. I want to get a Valentine for Cameron. Speaking of, what do I do about Cameron and Christmas?"

I examined one of the bear ornaments on the window display tree. "What kind of present do you want to give him?"

I chose three bear ornaments and put them in my cart. One was a bear lying in a boat and fishing, another was a bear bundled up in winter gear from head to toe, and one was a bear caroling.

"What do you mean, what kind?"

"Well, a funny gift, a sweet gift, something practical — maybe you could get him guitar strings. His are always breaking."

"But what if I get him guitar strings and he gets me something like earrings?"

"So he gets you earrings," I said.

"Earrings mean something more than guitar strings … Sadie, stop laughing at me."

I choked back my laughter. "Ruth, don't you think you and Cameron should talk sometime? Figure out what's going on with you two?"

"Are you kidding? I'd rather swim in a sea of alligators."

"Alligators don't swim in the sea."

"And you're one to talk. What are you getting Andrew?"

I winced and turned away from her so she wouldn't see. Andrew. My ex-friend.

I grabbed Ruth's elbow. "Frankie."

Ruth looked around. "What, she's here?"

"No. We need to get her a present."

"Why are you so worried about Frankie all of a sudden?"

"I don't know, Ruth ... oh okay!" I blurted. I couldn't hold it in. I told her everything Andrew had said. Then I sat down on a bench and dug my toes into the floor. I couldn't explain what was going on with me.

"Sadie." Ruth sat down next to me. "Andrew overreacted. He's drastic sometimes. And yes, Frankie has been different lately. But maybe you're overreacting too? You know how Frankie is. Tomorrow she could decide she hates us, and what then?"

"Lately, I've gotten this feeling, this really strong feeling, that I have to do something. I felt that way about going with you to talk to Doug. And I felt that way about bringing Frankie out to the cabin. I can't explain it, Ruth ..."

Ruth stopped picking her fingernail and studied my face. After a long minute, she nodded. "I never thought about other people having that feeling."

I frowned at her. Were we talking about the same feeling? Just like on Thanksgiving, I felt on the edge of plummeting over a cliff. My real thoughts and feelings were under control, hidden, but if I stepped the tiniest bit further, nothing would be safe. Ruth would see me. The risk was almost worth it, if Ruth felt the same things I did. But what if she didn't? What if I told her I thought God was asking me to do things, and she laughed at me?

Ruth went back to picking her fingernail. "When I was six, my family went to my grandparents' beach house in Maine. Grandpa had cancer, but I didn't know that. I just knew he wasn't feeling well. One morning at breakfast, Grandpa started coughing, and he couldn't stop. All the adults flurried around, and someone took him to the hospital. What I remember was running away, out the door onto the beach into a wild, windy day. Sand stung my cheeks, and wind filled my jacket so that my feet lifted off the sand and I literally flew backwards. I fought my way across the sand, ripped off my shoes, and kicked my way into the water, not caring that the bottoms of my jeans were soaked. I couldn't breathe. I cried and cried and pounded the air with my fists. It felt solid, Sadie, like I was beating on my dad's chest. I kicked and sobbed until I was exhausted. And then warmth slid across my shoulders. Warmth, Sadie, when my toes were in ten degree water. I opened my eyes and saw that the sky had opened up. Sun streamed through the clouds, so bright the light was almost golden. Sand glinted in the air, swirling around me. The wind blew, but now I was caught in a whirlwind of warm, golden air. That was the first time I had the feeling, Sadie. I knew, one hundred percent, God was there."

I hadn't had to plunge. Ruth had done it for me. "Does God ask people to do things?"

"Sure. I think people just have to learn to listen."

We sat there, silent, for a long moment.

"Ruth," I finally said.

"Yep?"

"Thank you. Talking about ..." My voice trailed off.

"I know. It feels strange talking about God in public. Like you're sharing something super-private. It is private, I guess. But when I hear Doug talk about God, or Dad even, or especially Mark or Hannah, I see God in ways I couldn't see on my own. So I think it's good. To talk about God, I mean." Ruth shrugged and then grinned. "So. What would Frankie like for Christmas?"

I couldn't help grinning back. "Obviously she would want a bear ornament."

Ruth laughed. "So, are you ready to hit the stocking stuffers?"

"That has to be where the clue is." I followed Ruth to the stocking stuffer bins near the back wall of the store. We sorted through mini toys, moose keychains, glasses repair kits, colored pencils, Slinkies, and Life Savers Sweet Story Books. No origami shape appeared. We dug for a little longer.

"Maybe someone picked it up," Ruth said. "We can ask at the desk."

Ruth settled on a tie for her dad's Sunday morning collection, one with a very intellectual moose who wore eyeglasses and read from a book. She found wrap-around earphones for her mom, who constantly lost her earphones when she went running.

"For Cameron, I'll look at The Fray website. Maybe they have a signed something."

"He'd like that." I shifted my heavier-by-the-minute basket to the other arm. I'd picked up a mini camera tripod for Dad. Now I had Pips, Frankie, and Ruth, who I couldn't shop for right now, and I didn't even want to think about Andrew.

"Lost something, girls?" Henry, Moose Track's shop-keeper, frowned at the mess we'd made of his bins.

"Did you see my parents come in and leave origami here, by any chance?" I asked.

"No, haven't seen your parents for days," Henry said with no hint of a lie in his eyes.

"How about Andrew Baxter?" Ruth dug her elbow into my side.

Henry shook his head. "Nope, sorry."

As Henry walked away, my stomach churned. Maybe the Advent calendar *had* been from Andrew all along. Maybe after the run-in with Frankie, he'd decided not to drop off the clue.

Ruth shrugged. "Oh well. You'll be able to figure the map out with one piece missing."

"Henry would know if any of them came into the shop." I set my basket down and rubbed my sore arm. "What if the calendar is from Andrew, Ruth? And he's so mad at me, he didn't deliver the map?"

"I'm sure someone just picked it up." Ruth passed me a bottle of green nail polish. "A new color for Frankie's collection?"

I tried to push Andrew out of my mind. All this time, I'd known he hadn't given me the calendar, so why was I second-guessing myself now? "What does Frankie like, anyway?"

Ruth shrugged. "I guess we should find out."

The understatement of the year. How could I have no idea what Frankie liked? I knew so many things about what she didn't like. Me. Ruth. My family. Bears. Andrew.

"I think this is all for today," I said. "I need more time to think about everyone else."

"Me too," Ruth said.

We paid Henry, and I couldn't help looking regretfully back at the bins as we picked up our bags.

"Sadie, I'm sure it will show up later," Ruth said.

I wasn't sure. In fact, I was almost positive that even the map in the calendar might lead to nothing, like today's clue. If the map was from Andrew, anyway.

Icy air blew into our faces as we pushed through the door.

From: Sadie Douglas
To: Pippa Reynolds
Date: Tuesday, December 14, 6:43 PM
Subject: Re: perhaps a kitten?

Pips, I know your present isn't a kitten. But I'm starting to believe you about the calendar. It just seemed like so much more fun from you than from Mom and Dad. As long as it's not from Andrew. I won't be able to stand it if he gave me this amazing present and then decided he hates me because I'm friends with Frankie, and the clues lead to some empty snowbank.

Chapter 21

Melting Point

"Pass the blue glass." Frankie had her tray set out and ready before any of the rest of us.

Vivian had set up a folding table in her cement room that had three bare walls against which she tossed and shattered ceramics. One wall, however, housed shelves and neat storage bins of ceramic shards and the kiln.

The room was the perfect place to work for many reasons. We could easily clean up any spilled glass, and we were close to the kiln. But the main benefit of working in this room was the theatre lights strung across a pole along the length of the room. Pools of colored light streamed down, lighting the glass in amber, red, blue, and green, just like the lights would on the tree.

A space heater blasted dusty air into the otherwise freezing room. Hopefully, soon my fingers would be as warm as my toes.

Ruth handed Frankie the ziplock baggie of blue glass and set the other colors on the table—clear, green, light amber brown, and rich cola-bottle brown.

"Andrew set his alarm clock last night to wake him up at three o'clock in the morning so he could tumble the last set of glass," Ruth said.

"Why isn't he here?" Nick passed a baggie of amber glass to Georgia.

I knew, without looking, that Ruth and Frankie were both avoiding my eyes.

"He had things to do," I answered lamely and reached for the clear glass. I set a few of the larger glass pieces out on my tray. I hadn't planned what shapes I would make exactly. Just like cloud-gazing, I thought the ideas should come from the actual shapes, instead of the other way around. You can't decide to find an elephant surfing in the clouds and then choose the cloud that looks most like a surfboard.

One of my shapes was a triangle, rounded on all the edges, and another was an almost perfect circle—how had that happened in the breaking and polishing? The largest piece was wide on both sides and narrow in the middle. I moved the shapes around, considering a tree, a present, and then when I put the circle above the triangle, I knew. An angel.

I laid the body, head, and wings together on the tray, and then sprinkled the finely ground pieces across the forehead to suggest a halo. Many of the glass slivers were long and thin, so next, I pieced together a few snowflakes, breaking the pieces carefully to make angles and edges in the fine design.

"Leave it to Sadie to make gorgeous patterns," Ruth said. "I can't get anything to work."

I looked across the table at her tray. She had tried to create a Christmas tree out of green glass, but the shapes weren't cooperating. The small pieces she put on top of the tree weren't small enough, and the tree ended up looking like a random stack of glass.

Next to her, Frankie didn't seem to be trying to make the shape of anything at all. She'd pulled larger blue pieces of glass and sprinkled designs on them with the tiny ground pieces. She used a tiny paintbrush and a little water to keep everything in place.

I walked around the table to get a closer look. "Frankie, how did you get this idea?"

She shrugged. "My mom does something like this when she fuses glass in her studio."

She turned to the sink, but not before a strange expression crossed her face. Raised eyebrows, her mouth slightly open, as though she had surprised herself.

Frankie turned on the water. "She uses glue though, so it probably won't work."

"I bet it will." Ruth stood over Frankie's creations, examining each one. "Frankie, will you help me with my ornaments?"

When Frankie turned back around, she avoided my eyes. No one could say that Frankie and I were really friends —

not yet. A thick wall between us kept each of us safe. Plenty of topics were off-limits, but sometimes, like now, cracks started to show. Frankie hadn't meant to bring up her mom. Of all the subjects I'd least want to discuss with Frankie, my mom topped my own list, too. Interesting. Maybe we had more in common than I thought.

Frankie and Ruth worked together on ornaments until we had all filled our trays. Vivian helped us load them into the kiln and then we went to the living room to eat egg rolls, chow mein, and cashew chicken.

No one knew what to talk about over dinner. As the silence started to feel awkward, Vivian jumped up and switched off the lights.

"So, my favorite part of this window is the stargazing," she said. "I figure that if long ago sailors and royalty and astronomers could invent constellations, I can too. I find pictures in the sky and make up stories to go with them. Like there, for instance." She pointed to a line of stars with a clump at one end. "To me, those stars look like a roller coaster. Maybe a giant amusement park waits for us in outer space."

"And they serve frozen stardust cones," Ruth added.

"And the most frightening ride of all is the ferris wheel." Frankie pointed to a circle of stars near Vivian's roller coaster. "Because if it stalls out at the top, you have to look down through galaxies and galaxies with nothing beneath you."

Nick, Georgia, and Ruth took their plates to the window and created ride after ride. I looked over at Frankie who watched them from the couch, eating her cashew chicken.

I went over to join her. "Is your mom an artist?"

Frankie shrugged. "She's worked with blown and fused glass ever since she moved to New York, but her new ultra rich boyfriend bought her a gallery in September, so she thinks she can make a living now."

I finished my last bite of chow mein and set down my plate. "Do you visit her often?"

"Not ever. She used to live on people's couches and stuff, you know, the starving artist thing, so it didn't make sense for me to come."

Each answer was like a drip from a clogged faucet. Obviously, Frankie had a lot more to tell, but she wasn't sure whether to offer me the information. Something, maybe curiosity, or something more, made me want to keep Frankie talking. I remembered what I'd said to Andrew when I'd tried to explain about Frankie. Maybe she just needed a friend.

"What does her art look like?"

"She doesn't have to stick to one color, you know, because she uses new glass, not old recycled bottles. She does vases and lamps, just ..."

When Frankie trailed off, I couldn't help asking, "What?"

"She acts like she's some amazing artist, you know, like her art is more important than anything. She and Dad aren't even divorced."

Before I could answer, Frankie spoke over me, not stopping now, as though she'd held all these words like a breath, and now that she had started to exhale, she couldn't stop the rest from tumbling out.

"She sent me home with divorce papers to give Dad, and she wants custody of me so I can live with her and her boyfriend in New York. Dad thinks I want to go, and he won't listen to me when I say I want to stay here. No one will. Ty and the girls, everyone, they think I want to go, all because of my stupid haircut. As though Mom gave me a choice about the dumb spa day. I'm still the same person, and they act like I'm totally different."

Frankie's anger made sense now, her embarrassment over her hair, her designer clothes, her trouble with her friends. I tried to think of something to say, but everything I thought of seemed like a pat on the head, when Frankie needed something more, something that made it clear I had heard her, and even if I didn't totally understand, I did care.

"I'm afraid I'll have to move soon, too," I said. "When I first came, I thought I would love it here, and then I was sure I'd hate it—"

The corner of Frankie's mouth turned up in an apologetic smile. "That was my fault."

"But now this feels like home."

"Won't the DNR keep your dad around at least until they work out the Patch thing?"

"I guess so. If she lives until spring," I said, and then stopped, remembering who I was talking to. I'd almost forgotten this was Frankie, and that her dad was Patch's worst enemy.

Frankie watched me, her eyes searching my face. "Patch is dangerous, Sadie. You haven't been around the bears very long, so maybe you don't understand—"

"You don't understand." The angry words burst out of my mouth before I could stop them. "People like your dad stalk the bears so they have to run for their lives all hunting season. Now, even when Patch is hibernating your dad is looking for her den. We have to check on her just to be sure he hasn't shot her in her sleep!"

"So you've been hiking out to her den?" Frankie asked.

Her question took my breath away. Why had I said all of that? I tried to make out her expression in the dark. "Frankie, you can't ..."

"Don't, Sadie," she said. "Let's just forget about this conversation, okay?"

But how could I forget when the echo of gunshots filled my head?

From: Sadie Douglas
To: Pippa Reynolds
Date: Wednesday, December 15, 6:43 PM
Subject: Re: hats

No. I won't forgive you if you don't wear the hats. I don't care how dumb Andrea says they are. It's tradition. I'm making Ruth wear one too on Friday. But I doubt Frankie will join us.

Still, Frankie is coming to youth group with us tomorrow. I can't figure out what to give her. And, of course, Andrew still isn't talking to me, so I guess I'm not giving him anything.

I ate a candy cane at lunch today in your honor. Give Cocoa a kiss for me.

Chapter 22

The Family in the Woods

I watched Frankie take it all in, the treehouse, the rope ladder, the turrets and chimes, and Penny with her teal spiked hair. Somehow, I had to talk to her about not telling her dad what I had said about Patch. I didn't know if I had actually given Patch away or not, but Frankie knew too much, either way, especially if she knew about the family in the woods.

"Hold this while I climb up?" She handed me the shoebox of carefully wrapped ornaments.

I took the box, climbed a few rungs up after her, and passed it off when she reached back down. Ruth and I joined her on the deck and introduced Frankie to Penny.

"Welcome," Penny said. "Gingerbread cookies and all the fixings tonight. You get to decorate the cookies yourselves."

"Not what I'd expect from church," Frankie said.

We went inside. Gingerbread cookies of every shape and character were set out on trays. I chose a reindeer. Ruth chose a star, and Frankie chose a tree. We swirled frosting onto our cookies and added red hots and silver sprinkles in patterns. I used mini black M&M's for my reindeer's eyes, and Frankie painted a star with yellow frosting at the top of her tree.

"Maybe you should come take an art class with me, with Vivian," I said to Frankie, trying to lighten everyone's mood.

Ruth poked at the glops of frosting that had come out too fast on her ornament. "No invitation for me? Thanks a lot. I'm an art failure." She stopped poking and took a bite. "At least I have more frosting than either of you."

We compared frosting on our way to three beanbags on the floor, and I had one of those moments where I see myself as though from a camera, a few feet away. Three girls, seeming to have fun at Christmas, bringing back their ornaments they had made together. No one would guess that Frankie and I had bitterly disliked each other all fall, and that even now, she might have told her dad about Patch's den, totally betraying my trust. But she'd made no promises, and I'd been careless. I should have listened to Andrew.

Ruth melted into her dreamy smile when Cameron started to play. Frankie noticed, but she just poked Ruth and smiled teasingly, nothing like she might have done just a few months ago. At least Ruth and Frankie seemed like they were becoming real friends. I closed my eyes and felt the drumbeat thud against my lungs. I didn't like to sing in public, so though most people sang along, I always just listened to the words. Tonight, Cameron and the boys had arranged a medley of Christmas carols, and the military beat of "The Little Drummer Boy" blended into the softer rhythm of "O Little Town of Bethlehem" which faded away into "Silent Night." As the music slowed and then stopped, I kept my eyes closed.

I sat there, thinking about Mom, healthy for most of December, decorating the house, making cookies. Frankie's mom, so far away in New York, made art out of glass and wanted Frankie to come live with her. After being away from her mom for so long, Frankie must feel horrible: wanting to go live with her mom because she missed her, but also wanting to stay with her dad, who she'd been with for all of this time.

"So." Doug's voice brought me back to the treehouse and away from my thoughts. "We've found a family to whom we'd like to bring Christmas."

Everyone started talking, and Ruth leaned over Frankie to whisper, "I can't wait, Sadie. Doug checked them out and thinks they'll be perfect."

"Checked who out?" Frankie asked.

Ruth turned her attention back to Doug as she answered, "This family in the woods."

Frankie grabbed Ruth's arm. "What family?"

"Ouch!" Ruth yelped.

"Ruth, why don't you come up and tell us a little more about the family that you and Sadie discovered," Doug said.

Ruth threw a confused glance at Frankie as she pulled her arm away. Frankie looked over at me, her question clear on her face. My stomach filled with nervous energy as thoughts came together, fast and uncontrollable. Frankie knew about the family in the woods. How could I not have seen that? I had known her dad knew about them. Now, she looked furious about Ruth announcing their presence in the woods to the youth group.

Ruth began, "Sadie and I found a family. A little girl about eight years old and a baby with their mom and dad living in an abandoned shack in the woods. We think—"

Frankie leapt to her feet. "That family is none of your business. Leave them alone."

Ruth stared at Frankie, and I watched them both, too surprised to react. For once, Doug didn't seem to know what to say either.

Penny broke the frozen silence. "Doug, why don't I chat with the girls, and you can move on with the other preparations?"

"Right," Doug said. "Sounds good."

Penny led Frankie and Ruth outside, and I followed them down the rope ladder, across the snowy yard, and into her tiny office. Frankie carried the shoebox the whole way, and I could see from the whiteness around her knuckles that her grip was deathly tight. No one said anything. When Penny closed the door, Frankie slumped into a chair, her old attitude and posture back.

"Frankie, I don't ..." Ruth began, but then her voice trailed off. Neither of us wanted to cross Frankie while she wore that expression.

Penny looked at Frankie, then at Ruth, and then at me. "Okay, I'll go first, then." She sat cross-legged on Doug's desk. "Out at the shack yesterday, Doug and I spoke to Quinn and Robin Thompson and their daughter, Roxy. Apparently, they'd been living out of their car until they accepted a job surveying the forest. A man, who is finalizing his purchase of the land, offered them the shack in exchange for their work. Why anyone needs the forest surveyed midwinter is beyond me, but I didn't ask. A shack may be cold in the winter, but it's much better than a car."

"They just want a home to live in," Frankie said. "Why can't you just leave them alone?" She turned on me. "Why didn't you tell me you knew about them?"

"I didn't realize you ..." My words trailed off. Maybe I hadn't known Frankie knew about the family, but I'd been pretty sure her dad did.

"You've ruined everything. Dad was barely willing to give them the shack before. The one thing they had to do was keep quiet. Now you're blabbing about them to everyone, and Dad will kick them out, and they'll be back in that freezing car for Christmas. Nice work, Sadie."

"But I didn't ..." While Frankie's anger crystallized into clear, angry words, my confusion became foggier with each second. I hadn't told her about the family because of Patch, because I hadn't wanted her dad to know about Patch's den.

"You know, it's like you care more about bears than you do about people. You're so worried about keeping Patch safe, you don't consider what finding her means to those people."

"What does it mean, Frankie?" I asked, not wanting to hear the answer.

"It means he'll give them the shack," she said, not looking at me. "Roxy found a bear den, but she wasn't sure if the bear was Patch. It could have been any hibernating bear. Then last night, when you told me that you'd been walking out past Patch's den, I knew." She looked up at me, her eyes hopeless and angry and trapped. "I just ... He has to give them that house, Sadie."

"So what, you're going to give Patch away to your dad?"

Frankie hugged the box to her chest. "I didn't say that."

But she hadn't denied it either.

"Girls," Penny said, reminding us that she and Ruth were in the room.

"Frankie, your dad did a very generous thing, offering to give the shack to the Thompson's after he buys that parcel of land. You never know, having a few more people know about the deal might be the very thing he needs to ensure that he follows through."

Frankie shrugged, took out her cell phone and sent a text. Even Penny couldn't pull her into a conversation now. Frankie's phone beeped with a new text.

"My dad's on his way. I'm out of here." She slammed the door on her way out.

I stood to follow her, but Penny caught my arm and said, "Why don't you let her cool down first?"

I looked from her to Ruth and back again. I hated not doing anything. I hated knowing that whatever happened to Patch was all my fault.

From: Sadie Douglas
To: Pippa Reynolds
Date: Thursday, December 16, 10:12 PM
Subject: Funny

So all this time I've been trying to figure out the perfect present for Frankie, and I finally came up with it tonight — a sketchbook, because she's a really good artist. But, it turns out that after pretending to be my friend for the past month, turns out she's never going to change. She told her dad about Patch behind my back. I never should have trusted her. We're not friends, and no way am I giving her a present. She only cares about herself and what she wants and she'll do anything to get it. I feel so dumb. Andrew was right all along.

Chapter 23

Layers

Dad passed me a plate filled with bacon and eggs. "Sadie, no, for the last time. You can't go sit out by Patch's den waiting for Jim Paulson to show up."

Higgins jumped up, and I didn't even stop him from stealing a piece of bacon from my plate. Mom pushed his paws off the table. "Down, Hig."

Dad and I had carried on this argument since Ruth's mom had dropped me off last night. "Dad, you don't understand. Jim Paulson is going to shoot her. Today. You can't just let him."

Dad sighed. "Look, Sadie, he might not know where the den is. By sitting out there, you'll only give him more information. And you can't guard Patch until spring."

I shoved my plate away and blinked back tears. "So we'll do nothing?"

Mom wrapped her arm around me and pulled me close, but instead of feeling comforted, I felt smothered. I didn't want hugs. I wanted to save Patch.

"I'll go to the research cabin today," Dad said. "We'll hike into the woods, and see what we can discover without giving Patch's den completely away. All right?"

"I saw Vivian at the grocery store yesterday," Mom said. "She hopes you'll come back for drawing lessons. Do you want me to call and see if she has time today?"

No dangled at the edge of my lips, but sitting at the kitchen table, suffocated in Mom's overly cheerful hug and fuming at Dad, the chance to be anywhere but home appealed to me. "Yeah. Okay, sure."

I went upstairs to grab my backpack. On my desk, the Advent calendar sat, today's drawer still unopened. All the anger and worry which shuddered through me focused on the calendar, and I grabbed it and hurled it across the room. The wood splintered at the top, and I kicked it for good measure. I wasn't a kid anymore, and no tree with painted pictures and little mysterious pieces of map inside could change the fact that the bear I loved would be shot in her sleep. Andrew was right. Being shut out was worst of all, worse even than trying to do something ourselves and failing. Everything I had done, all for the sake of doing the right thing — telling our parents about the family, telling Doug, trusting Frankie, all of it, had blown up in my face anyway. So much for doing the right thing, following the feeling I'd been so sure was God.

Thanks a lot. So nice of you to care.

I kicked the tree again and left it, broken against the wall. I left the Santa hats behind too.

Frankie didn't look at me once during school, which was fine by me. And I avoided Ruth. I hid in the library during lunch and ate alone. Talking to anyone would only turn to shouting, and most likely sobbing too. So much for celebrating the last day of school before break. Ms. Barton showed *The Grinch Who Stole Christmas* during the last two hours of the day, and I found myself chanting along, *I hate Christmas. Christmas stinks.*

Mom waited for me at the curb. "Off to Vivian's. She had time."

I didn't know how to feel about this. I'd rather be at Vivian's house than at home, but most of me, my mind, my heart, curled up next to Patch in the woods.

Mom chattered about next week's preparation for Christmas—decorating cards, wrapping presents, stuffing Dad's stocking, mailing gifts to relatives. I could only nod, choking back tears. *Patch could be dead now.* All I could see was her trusting brown eyes, the glance over her shoulder at Andrew and me as she led us to her den last fall. Maybe it hadn't been a trusting glance. Maybe I was imposing human thoughts and feelings on her like Dad always warned me not to do. *They aren't people, Sadie. They're wild animals.* Still, I felt connected to her. I loved her. And today, because of my bad decisions, she would die. When we finally arrived at Vivian's, I forced a smile. "Thanks, Mom."

I hurried out of the car, thankful that the icy air froze my tears before they rolled down my cheeks.

When Vivian opened the door, she took one look at me and said, "To the blue room."

I allowed myself to be marched down the hall and into my favorite room in Vivian's house, with three glass walls looking out to the snowbank beyond, and the one wooden wall painted indigo blue, decorated with glow-in-the-dark stars. Vivian had already set out mugs of steaming hot cocoa and Santa cookies with red frosted hats, coconut beards and eyebrows, half a maraschino cherry for a nose, and two blue M&M's for eyes.

"May I look at your sketchbook?" Vivian asked.

I passed over my sketchbook and watched her turn pages. Copies of *Starry Night* and the magical realism images filled the first pages. From there, my sketchbook exploded with sketches, doodles, lists of words. Vastly different than capital A art, this messy collection of thought had spilled out with little planning. I'd drawn a series of Mom cartoons as she zoomed around the house, decorating. A caped figure delivering a box to my porch in early morning light filled a double page spread. Patch, yawning, stepped out of her den in spring, and on the next page, Frankie and Ruth laughed together over their ornaments.

"Sadie, I'm so proud of you," Vivian said, passing the sketchbook back to me. "You let go of trying to do it right, and just started drawing."

Why couldn't life be like my drawing then? Because

everywhere else I had tried too hard to get it right, only to get it very, very wrong.

Vivian opened her sketchbook. "Let's talk about layering, and then we'll draw and talk."

I nodded. My need to talk boiled up and threatened to spill out, but I fought back. Words couldn't help Patch. Even though I couldn't stand the sickness in my stomach, even though I might explode if I didn't escape the guilt and frustration and disappointment and sadness, the thought of doing anything to soothe myself seemed wrong, selfish. I had betrayed Patch. I had tried to do the right thing, but I'd been all wrong, and now her death would be all my fault.

"Every drawing starts with base shapes—we've talked about that a lot." Vivian drew a circle next to a square with rounded corners. "But we haven't talked about how a drawing develops. If you stick with a piece, restating your lines, shading, adding layers and details, you find something richer than if you turn the page and start fresh."

I frowned across the table at her. "I prefer starting fresh."

"Me too." Vivian smiled down at her page as she added rounded ears to her doodle. "I like the idea of a fresh start with no mistakes. But by starting over fresh, you leave something important behind."

"Just mistakes. Can't you take what you learned to the new page?" I asked.

"Yes, absolutely. But you're at the point where working with your mistakes, pushing yourself beyond what's easy, will help you."

I sighed and opened my sketchbook to a clean page.

"Choose one you've already started." Vivian paged through her drawings. "I will too."

I flipped page after page, and stopped on Patch. I couldn't think about anything else, anyway. I retraced my lines, not sure what to add.

Vivian had chosen a picture of me, biting my lip as I drew in her blue room. "Here I could add to the background, detail the images, or superimpose an element that wasn't there to begin with. Such as an audience cheering you on as you draw, or the stars peeking down from the sky to see your stroke marks, anything. Sometimes I close my eyes to see what a picture needs."

I looked at my drawing of Patch's den and closed my eyes. What did I see? Hunters, surrounding her den, closing her in. I didn't want to draw them, so instead I sketched trees, strong, solid, guardian trees, posted all around. Still, Frankie slipped into my charcoal forest, reminding me of the danger.

"So, Frankie was only pretending to be my friend." I slashed at my page, making angular branches. "Everyone warned me not to trust her, but I didn't listen. I never listen."

Vivian kept drawing, giving me room and space to keep talking.

"And now, because of me, Patch is going to be murdered." Tears dripped onto my sketchbook, and the water smeared the graphite. I swept through to the first blank page.

"Try something for me, Sadie." Vivian reached for my

160

sketchbook and found my water-streaked page. "Try sticking with this drawing, no matter what happens."

I rolled my eyes, and picked up a paper towel to scrub at the stains. A blurred, watercolor-like effect began on my page.

Vivian watched over my shoulder. "There's something I hadn't expected."

I studied the lines, the way some blended smoothly into the others, and the way others stood out, choppy and rough. Patch's cheek and ear had blurred, making it appear as though she shook her head as she yawned and took in the sunrise. The soft edges against the rough ones were like the pain that both melted and stabbed inside me.

And suddenly, looking at Patch's eye, I crumbled. An involuntary sob ripped through me, doubling me over with the pain. I wanted to run and hide and scream and throw anything I could find against the walls, but I couldn't release my arms which hugged tight against my body. "It's too much," I choked out. "I can't save her. They won't let me save her."

Vivian's arms circled around me, but her hug didn't feel like Mom's. This hug wasn't protective, pretending to shield me from the world and all of the hurt from which no one could protect me. This was a hug with no lies in it, a hug of *I know. This hurts. It's okay to cry.*

I rocked there, knotted up on my stool, with Vivian holding me for what felt like hours. And then Vivian's phone rang. To me, it sounded like a bell tolling on an old-time church, the signal of death. Another sob racked through me, and Vivian let it ring. But when the caller hung up on the answering machine and called again, Vivian lifted me gently to my feet.

"I should answer." With her hand on my back, she led me to the phone. "Hello?"

A voice I hadn't expected tumbled out from the other end of the line.

"Wait, slow down, Frankie. Yes, Sadie is right here." Vivian held the phone out to me, but I motioned for her to listen too. I couldn't do this on my own.

Frankie's voice tumbled across the phone line. "He's on his way over there now, to the shack, to convince Quinn Thompson to kill the bear. Then he's going to blame it all on Quinn, and Dad isn't giving them the shack. Maybe he would have, but Dad says Quinn talks too much. He's afraid Patch's death will be traced back and blamed on him, and he'll lose his hunting license. And the only thing I could think of was to find witnesses, lots and lots of witnesses, so Dad can't go back on his word. Sadie, you have to go out there. Someone has to catch Dad with Quinn. Take your dad and Helen and Meredith and anyone else you can find. Please, Sadie. Roxy ..."

And then Frankie started crying. My mind stalled in confusion. Frankie didn't cry. And she didn't care if her dad or Quinn or anyone else shot Patch. I should be the one crying.

"Sadie, Roxy believes her family will have a new life," Frankie choked out over her tears. "But Dad is sending them back to live in a car."

Vivian recovered first. "Yes, Frankie. We'll call out to the research cabin and let Matthew and Helen know that your dad is on his way. We'll go out there ourselves right now, too. If there's anything we can do, we'll do it."

Frankie sniffed and then whispered, "Thank you," and hung up.

Vivian grabbed her cell phone and handed me the cordless. "Call every number you know."

We both dialed madly for a few minutes, catching Andrew on his house phone and Dad on his cell. Dad and Helen were just on the cabin front steps, back from their trip into the woods.

"We'll head back on the ATV's," Dad said. "No time to worry about Patch and the noise."

I heard Andrew shout, "I'm coming too."

I couldn't stand waiting here at Vivian's, yet again, left out of the action. She nodded. "We'll load up Peter's ATV in the truck. The ATV will hold us both, and we can follow your dad, Helen, and Andrew out to the den."

Chapter 24

Just One Shot

Loading up the ATV was easier said than done. We carefully drove it up a long ramp made for this purpose, but the tires kept slipping off. Finally, we managed to push it the last few inches, fold up the ramp so it fit in the truck bed, and slam the tail gate.

Vivian, usually a casual driver, took the snowy corners so fast I thought we might slide off the road. Still, I couldn't keep my legs from bouncing nervously as we drove. *Please don't let us be too late. Please, just this once, let something work out.* We roared up the research station driveway, maneuvered the ATV down off the truck, and sped into the trees, using the tracks Dad and Helen had already plowed with their tire treads.

Vivian cut the engine when we came close enough to see smoke billowing out of the shack's chimney. We approached in a lower, quieter gear. I held my breath, listening for gunshots, until we reached the thick line of bushes, jumped down off the ATV, and shoved through. I almost sobbed with relief. Dad, Helen, Andrew, the Thompsons, and Jim all stood hands on hips, yelling. Jim couldn't look that mad, I was sure, if he'd already shot Patch. But then Frankie's words came back to me. Jim didn't want to have witnesses. He might be just as mad to be caught after the shooting, maybe even more so. *Please let her still be okay. I can't live with myself if she dies.*

Andrew looked up and over at me. I knew then, because of his dry eyes, that Patch was still alive. But from his grim expression, I knew the danger wasn't over yet. Vivian and I slipped and slid down the snowy embankment to join the group.

Jim looked up. "More trespassers, I see."

"Jim, as far as I know, this isn't your land yet," Helen said, her voice sounding tired, as though she had repeated this statement many times already.

Jim raised his hands, as though he was the victim here. "Look, close enough. The land's in escrow. Still, if you're going to fuss over a dangerous bear, I'll go through official channels. Call the DNR. Whatever. That bear's a threat, and I want it off my land. As far as I'm concerned, that bear has earned her one-way ticket out of Owl Creek. I don't care how it's done."

"But the DNR doesn't kill bears during hibernation." I couldn't keep my mouth shut.

Dad shot me a warning look.

165

"No, sweetheart." Jim's voice dripped with sarcasm. "But they can certainly take her into captivity. Much easier now, while she's hibernating, than in the spring when we'd have to find her first."

"But that's dangerous," I said, turning to Helen. "Isn't it? Didn't you say that bears sometimes die when they come out of hibernation too soon? And what about her cubs?"

"Cubs?" the little girl, Roxy, whispered.

I hadn't noticed her there, peeking out from behind her dad's leg. Her huge eyes were round and dark with fear. There, clutching her dad's leg, she looked even smaller than she had before. She hadn't known. Of course she hadn't— she was just a kid, maybe eight years old. Her parents talked about finding the bear as though the search was a trea-sure hunt. Roxy hadn't understood that her dad planned to kill the bear. Still, no matter how small she looked, if Roxy hadn't followed us, maybe none of this would have happened.

Dad crossed his arms and narrowed his eyes at Jim. "Call the DNR. Just make sure nothing happens to that bear in the meantime. Because I guarantee you, if she ends up with even a scratch, I will make sure the DNR removes your hunting license for good. That's a promise."

"And if you don't get off my land with those ATV's of yours," Jim said. "I'll call the police and have you all arrested for trespassing."

Helen and Dad faced off with Jim for a few more moments and then turned to go. No one seemed to have anything more to say. I hated to leave, knowing that Jim could go shoot Patch right now if he wanted to. I held on to the hope that Frankie was right, that losing his hunting license was enough of a threat. But Patch was obviously still in danger if Jim already owned this land. And how could he? How long did it take to buy land anyway?

As I turned to go, Roxy caught my hand, her grip sharp as always.

"You have to help the bears," she whispered. "I didn't know they would hurt them."

"Kill them." The words shot from my mouth like poison darts before I could stop them.

Roxy's eyes filled with tears, and my lungs tightened with the pain of yet one more mistake to add to my collection.

"Leave my little girl alone," Quinn Thompson said, taking her hand protectively as though she wasn't the one grabbing onto me.

I stumbled away, not able to look at Vivian or Dad, not able to even look at Andrew or Helen. I buckled into the ATV and hid my face against my knees so no one could see the shame burning in my cheeks.

From: Sadie Douglas
To: Pippa Reynolds
Date: Saturday, December 18, 3:26 PM
Subject: Re: Hats???

Sorry, Pips. I couldn't write yesterday. Everything is a mess, and we're going to have a meeting on Tuesday to decide if Patch is a category two bear, and if she is, Jim is going to force the DNR to take her out of hibernation, and Helen is pretty sure that will kill her. And her cubs, too. I didn't wear a hat. I'm sorry. I just didn't feel up to it.

From: Sadie Douglas
To: Pippa Reynolds
Date: Sunday, December 19, 1:46 PM
Subject: Present

Mom put my present to you in the mail today. I hope you like it. It's not an Advent calendar or a kitten, but it's handmade, the way presents should be, right? I wish you were here, Pips. I feel so bad thinking about Patch dying and it being my fault. Mom is starting to slow down too, like the holiday spirit has all run out and she's just drained. Just in time for Christmas. But of course, she won't admit anything is wrong.

From: Sadie Douglas
To: Pippa Reynolds
Date: Monday, December 20, 8:21 PM
Subject: Meeting tomorrow

Tomorrow's the meeting. Pray for Patch, Pips. I want to believe she has a chance, but I'm afraid it's just too late.

Chapter 25

Marble Eyes

The moose head stared, his cold marble eyes offering no forgiveness to the shouting crowd who'd gathered at DNR headquarters for the meeting. The tension coiled tightly around me, wrapping dark fingers around my throat. Somehow, I had believed this was over, this anger, everyone fighting with everyone else.

Don't be foolish, Sadie.

I had painted a mental picture of a perfect Owl Creek, the bears and hunters and Mom and Dad and me all safe and happy and okay. I knew all the time I held that picture that it was impossible. Mom would still be sick, Jim would still be a hunter, and people would still argue. But now, with anger thick like vicious scribbles across my naïve picture, I felt even more miserable than if I hadn't hoped at all.

Beside me, Dad held Mom's hand, looking anything

but relaxed. Mom had insisted on coming, even though we all knew she didn't feel well. Helen sat on my other side, her muscles so tense she might spring from her seat at any minute. She'd offered to switch with me so I could sit by Andrew, but we'd both mumbled excuses and avoided one another's eyes. Why make a terrible night worse?

Meredith's ranger uniform was pressed as always. Still, her white-knuckled grip on the front podium gave away her frustration. She held up her hands yet again, and slowly, a sullen silence spread over the group as everyone found a seat.

Meredith cleared her throat. I'd never seen her nervous before, but then, Helen or Dad had always been the ones facing the angry crowd. Now Meredith had to stand up to them herself.

She gripped the podium again. "Originally, this meeting was called to discuss Helen's research, but due to recent developments, Patch and her yearlings will be our topic of concern."

Jim Paulson stood. "For the record, I want to point out the absurdity of discussing what I do with my own property."

Mack Jefferson, who never seemed to leave Jim Paulson's side, stood up next to him. "I'm tired of DNR giving more and more rules. Why can't you just let us be?"

The room erupted into argument again, most in agreement with Jim, yelling at Meredith.

"Listen to me." Holding up her hands was becoming a comically ineffective gesture. Meredith didn't have the slightest measure of control over this crowd. When they finally settled enough so she could be heard, she continued. "No one mentioned new rules. Bears are already a protected species. You can't just remove four bears from hibernation, take them out of the wild, just because you want to."

"No, because that would cost the state too much money." Mack sat and crossed his arms, as though his case was closed.

"I've offered to dispose of them instead of sending them into state protection," Jim said. "But Matthew Douglas assures me I'll lose my hunting license for my trouble."

Dispose of them. Jim Paulson made my skin crawl. How could he talk about the bears as though they were anything but beautiful, gentle creatures? Frankie sat on his other side, and I thought about her expression when she told me how much she loved her dad. Enough, I guess, to buy into his crazy ideas about bears being pests, disposable items.

"At this point in time, the DNR's rules state that a bear that bluff charges is a category three bear, a bear who can, in fact, be removed from a community. Jim's claim about Patch charging him last October puts her into that category. However, Patch is also a valuable research bear, and Helen's research has begun to show that bluff charges may be just that: bluffs. The DNR seeks irrefutable proof that Patch is a category three bear, by more than one account, before they will take on the expense of removing her and the three yearlings from the wild."

Mack jumped to his feet. "Well, let me count the ways. That bear has huffed and stamped and charged at me plenty of times."

171

"I'm sorry." Helen smiled tightly. "I'm afraid we'll need more specifics than that. When, where, and what exactly happened?"

For the rest of the hour, people told stories of encounters with Patch, most friendly, a few more worrisome. Once, Mary Hanson found Patch in her garage. Cornered, Patch charged out the door and knocked Mary over, her claws leaving behind a wicked scratch down Mary's arm.

"I don't think she meant to hurt me, though," Mary had insisted.

Still the damage was done. Between Mary's account, Mack's wild claims, and Jim's story, Patch was deemed a dangerous bear.

"Do something, Dad," I whispered to him. "Say something."

But Helen took my hand in both of hers and leaned down to say to me, "Sadie, we can't fight this official ruling. Arguing will only endanger my already shaky status as a scientist here. Your dad can't interfere with this process no matter how much he wants to without taking sides. Both of our jobs are on the line, and the safety of all the bears."

Andrew leaned forward and hissed. "Patch's one shot was to stay hidden. And you gave her away."

"Andrew!" Helen's sharp reprimand didn't keep the shame from rising into my throat, burning, driving the pain and anger deeper.

Yes. I had trusted Frankie even though everyone had warned me not to, and now Patch would pay for my mistake. Andrew's stony expression made me want to shake him, shake him until he stopped blocking me out. Maybe I deserved his anger, and maybe I had made mistakes, but didn't I feel badly enough? Wasn't it enough that Patch and the yearlings would probably die? Did Andrew have to hate me, too?

I clenched my fists and tried to hear what Meredith was saying, but the words, distorted by my fury, didn't connect fully. Something about Jim first bringing his signed land deed to the DNR, because removal during hibernation could only happen at the bequest of the landowner, and then something about tranquilizers and a zoo in Canada. So if Patch lived, she could look forward to life in the zoo, trapped, penned up. Still, I couldn't help closing my eyes. *Just let her live, God. Please. Let the bears make it.*

When I opened my eyes, I glanced over at Andrew. I don't know what I expected, maybe that he had caught onto the shreds of hope that maybe after all Patch would live this through. Andrew's face, though, was anything but hopeful. He scowled at Meredith, at Jim, and at Frankie, who was headed our way through the dispersing crowd of people.

I stood, hoping to disappear before Frankie passed our bench, but no such luck.

"Sadie," she called from behind me as I pushed down the row as quickly as I could manage without actually shoving anyone out of my way.

I stiffened and knew she'd see the rise of my shoulders, known that I had heard her. Still, I didn't care. Let Frankie think I was rude. She was a killer, and I didn't want to be friends with a killer anyway.

A white haired woman stood up in front of me. "Oh, excuse me, dear." She leaned over to pick up her purse, moving slower than I thought possible. I considered standing on the bench and leaping over the back into the next row when Frankie caught up with me.

"Sadie." She pulled my shoulder so that I had no choice but to turn toward her. She shoved the box of ornaments into my arms. "I forgot to give you these. And Sadie, thank you for helping me. I just ..."

Frankie's eyes filled with tears, shocking me for a moment, and then making me furious all over again. It was too late for her to cry, to try to be my friend, when everything had already gone so wrong.

"Leave me alone." I pulled away from her, thinking of everything I'd lost. Andrew. And now most likely Patch and the yearlings. And worse, I'd lost something bigger, something I couldn't exactly describe. I'd lost the warm fullness inside me that made me feel sure that the next decision was right. Now all I felt was jagged, painful edges, like my insides had been turned to glass and then shattered.

"Sadie, I thought if I told Dad, he'd still give the Thompson's the shack. But he isn't. He's throwing them out and—"

"And killing Patch too," I said.

"But Sadie," Frankie's eyebrows pulled together in the middle, as though she genuinely didn't understand. "Patch is just ..."

"Just a bear?" I asked. "Why did I ever think I could trust you?"

As I strode away, my insides broke apart all over again. I hated what I'd said, but meant it all the same. If only I could shove everyone in this room, everyone who had debated over Patch's life and stood by while an innocent, gentle bear—everyone knew she wouldn't hurt anyone really—was sentenced to either death or life in a zoo. To my left, a man and woman discussed their grocery list for the week, and on my other side, someone talked about driving through the neighborhoods to see the Christmas lights. Christmas. As though anyone could think of that now.

Ruth stopped me on my way out, a small, sad look on her face. "Sadie, I'm so sorry."

"I can't talk, Ruth. If I talk ..." but I couldn't say more because tears already threatened.

I had to get out of this room, away from everyone, someplace where I could breathe. I turned toward the door, and that's when I saw Mom start to fall.

Chapter 26

Shattering

Watching Mom collapse is like watching a house of cards fall. Sometimes you don't even see what tiny breath of wind starts the destruction, when suddenly, with terrible fragility, the entire structure tumbles in on itself. People gasped, as they always do, and Jim Paulson, of all people, reached out for her before she hit the floor.

"Make some room," he called, ever the hero.

Dad and I rushed to her, but she was already out, eyelids fluttering, on the other side where Dad and I couldn't reach her. When Mom first started passing out like this, I used to tell myself that she had gone to a beautiful place of crystal and feathers, warm, and filled with golden sunlight, like the dreams you don't want to wake up from. Only then could I understand why she didn't come back to us, no matter how much we shook her or called her name.

Dad lifted Mom, like a broken bird, and carried her out to the Jeep. I opened the door, playing the role I've come to know so well, climbing in after Mom, to buckle her into the seat and sit next to her. I still held the shoebox Frankie had shoved into my arms.

Andrew, Helen, Ruth, and her dad had all followed us outside.

"Is there anything we can do?" Helen asked.

"Would you be willing to bring a change of clothes for us to the hospital?" Dad asked. "We're likely to be there overnight."

"And feed Higgins?" I called.

Helen nodded, and Dad backed out of the parking lot. I held Mom's limp hand as we sped toward the hospital, sitting close so she wouldn't fall over or hit her head. When we pulled up to the ER doors, orderlies rushed out with a gurney to collect Mom. Dad parked in the garage, and then we hurried inside, following directions down a hallway and up in an elevator, into a small exam room where nurses had hooked Mom up to an IV and a heart monitor.

I had carried the shoebox in with me, barely thinking. I hugged it close as the flurry of activity finished, and the familiar hospital scene settled around me. The rhythmic beep of the heart monitor, the antiseptic smell, and Dad talking quietly to the nurses mixed with the white noise of the heating system. And the heat. Like all hospital rooms, this one was too hot, the stuffy air too thick to breathe.

"I'm going outside."

Dad turned from the nurse and frowned. "What?"

"Just for some air." I was already halfway out the door.

"Stay here," Dad said. "They might move Mom. You know the drill."

But I couldn't stay, and I couldn't explain this to him either. I just had to get out of that building, out into the fresh air. I looked down at the box in my arms. "I'll just put the ornaments in the Jeep. I'll be right back."

Dad sighed, but handed me the keys. "Right back, Sadie. I don't want to have to worry about you, too."

No. We wouldn't want that.

As soon as the door clicked shut behind me, I started to jog, and once I found the stairwell, I started to run. I ran down flight after flight to the ground floor, and then crashed out through the lobby. Who cared what anyone thought of a seventh grader running through the hospital lobby? People must have run through before, grief-stricken, joyful, confused, like me.

The automatic doors opened, and I bolted through onto the snow-covered steps. Immediately I started slipping and sliding, but I kept on running. I needed to finally breathe. When I stepped on the bottom step, my boot slid on an icy patch, and the box flew out of my hand. It hit the ground with a disturbing crash. Our ornaments. The ornaments Frankie, Ruth, and I and the others had made. The ornaments even Andrew had helped with. All for the family in the shack, for Roxy. And she'd given Patch to the hunters. Suddenly I hated that box and everything it stood for. I kicked it across the sidewalk, and then ran through the snow to kick it and kick it again. When it lodged into the snowbank at the edge of the street, I stomped and pounded on the box until the snow had soaked it through and the box was almost flattened, until my breath came in ragged sobs.

And then I stopped. The destroyed box swum before my tear-filled eyes, the red cardboard staining the snow pink. I scooped it up and stumbled toward the parking garage, avoiding the eyes of the few passersby in the night. I unlocked the Jeep and climbed into the backseat, still cradling the box. My sobs started fresh as I set the box down, and pulled away the disintegrating lid, saw the broken glass inside.

I break everything. No matter what I do, or how hard I try, everything, everyone around me breaks.

I took out three clear shards and tried to arrange them in my palm so that they matched one another. A sharp edge sliced my pinky, but I ignored this and kept trying to match the edges. One way and then another, the word *broken* repeating through my mind over and over.

I don't know how long I sat there in the dark, piecing the glass back together, choosing new pieces, finding no fits. Suddenly the door opened behind me, and I heard Andrew say my name and then gasp.

Again, sobs burst out of me, and I covered my face to hold in the sounds choking out of me. Something sharp pressed into my cheek, and I didn't understand why my face felt so warm and sticky and wet.

"Don't touch your face, Sadie," Andrew climbed up into the Jeep behind me and gently took my hands and looked down at them.

I looked down too, and saw that my hands were covered

with blood. In the moonlight, I could see slivers of glass that had wedged into my fingers and palms.

"Stay there," Andrew ordered. "Don't touch anything."

He jumped out and opened the front passenger door to look in the glove box. He found a napkin and brought it back. He dabbed at my cheek where it stung.

"You didn't cut your cheek badly, but we should have the doctors look at your hands."

"Patch will die." My mind was hazy and tears kept spilling down my cheeks. "I can't save her. I didn't listen to you, and it's all my fault."

Andrew put his hands on my shoulders and looked me in the eyes. "Sadie, it's not your fault. We all tried to help Patch."

"But I didn't listen to you about Frankie."

"It's not like I haven't let you down lately. Everyone makes mistakes, Sadie." He leaned forward and brushed away my tears. "I'm sorry, Sadie."

I just couldn't stop crying. "I'm sorry too," I whispered.

"We have to let Patch go," Andrew said.

Whatever remaining shreds of me that were still whole, shattered now as I felt the truth of Andrew's words, as I pictured Patch's limp body being pulled out of her den into the snow. One way or another, I had to let Patch go.

Andrew carefully helped me out of the Jeep. "Mom will be looking for us soon, I'm sure. Maybe we should go fix up your hands?"

I nodded and let him guide me into the bright lights of the ER waiting room.

Chapter 27

Into the Fire

After a nurse washed and bandaged my hands, scolding me that I should be more careful, Andrew texted his mom to let her know I was all right, and we went back upstairs. The doctors wanted to keep Mom for an extra twelve hours, so Helen offered to take me home.

Even though the sunrise was beautiful, the dark clouds streaked with burnt orange and golden yellow, I mostly stared at my bandaged hands on the way home. I felt like a limp rag, wrung out, and useless. Worse than useless because on top of everything that had gone wrong—Patch, Mom, Frankie—I had thrown a fit and broken ornaments that weren't mine to break. And now, a family whose life was even worse than mine would have a bare, depressing Christmas tree. Some send off as they were forced to move out of the shack.

But what bothered me most, even more than my mistakes, was the frightening broken edges of my insides, broken edges that didn't feel like they could ever heal. I thought of Ruth's story, of how she'd beat against the wind and known God was with her, and then of my own experience, how God reached out to comfort me as rain drummed on the Catholic church's roof. So why not now? Why did I feel broken beyond repair? Had one of my mistakes, or the collection of all of them, been too much?

Finally, when I couldn't stand the pressure of guilt burning inside me, I said, "Frankie's dad is still kicking Roxy and her family out of the shack after Christmas. And now they won't even have ornaments on their tree."

I looked up at Andrew, expecting a grim look in return, but instead, he gave me his crooked smile. "I missed out the first time, so I'll help you make new ones, if you want."

We'd left some glass behind at Vivian's house, since we hadn't needed it all for the first set of ornaments. A tiny breath of possibility slipped around the edges of the heaviness that pressed down on my chest. Could something, anything, from this miserable week be fixed?

I used Helen's cell phone to call Vivian, who said she'd fire the kiln so it would be hot and ready.

Helen promised to go check on Higgins after she dropped us at Vivian's house. Vivian had baked a fresh batch of Santa cookies and set them out in the concrete room on the table next to the baggies of glass and kiln trays.

"I'll leave you to your work," she said. "Call me when you're ready to fire the trays. I'll be in the blue room."

As she hurried away, Andrew picked up a triangular shape, and a long, thin spike of blue glass. "What am I supposed to make of this mess? Maybe this could be a spear?"

"No spears," I said.

"A trident, then." Andrew chose a few shorter pieces of glass and shaped a fork on top of the long spike.

Laughing, after all of that crying, was a relief. "No weapons."

"Maybe it's a fork. You have rules against utensils?"

I pushed together a collection of curvy shapes. "I'm making a reindeer."

"Show off." Andrew tossed the washcloth at me.

I tossed it back, making sure to hit him in the face.

He aimed at me, but I raised my bandaged hands. "You're picking on an injured person?"

He grinned and tossed anyway. "Absolutely."

We filled the trays with shapes of stars and bells and a few more complex arrangements such as my reindeer. In the end, we made about seventy ornaments in all. Vivian came in to help us load them into the kiln when the doorbell rang.

"Sadie, go see who that is, will you?" Vivian asked.

Frankie stood outside, Higgins wiggling in her arms. Helen's station wagon waited in the driveway. After Frankie pushed Higgins into my arms, she shoved her hands into her pockets and stared at her feet. Higgins arched back and forth to try to lick my nose. I scratched his ears, and as it became clear Frankie didn't intend to speak first, I finally said, "So ..."

"You don't have to help me," Frankie began.

I sighed. If I'd learned anything over the past few months, I'd learned Frankie never did anything without an underlying reason of her own.

"It's just that I ..." She shivered as her voice trailed off.

I sighed again. It was cold, and this didn't promise to be a short conversation. "Come in," I said, my voice not very welcoming.

Frankie looked up at me then, a question on her face. After a moment of looking at me, she shrugged, as though she hadn't found her answer but would press forward anyway. She came inside, took off her boots, coat, and hat, and went to sit in the living room where we'd sat just a few nights ago. Where I'd given away Patch's secret. I sat stiffly on a chair across from Frankie. Higgins jumped up, putting his paws on my knees until I gave in and pulled him into my lap. His fur was soft against my fingertips, the only part of my hands not bandaged.

"A couple days before Thanksgiving, just after I had come home from Mom's house, Dad and Mack loaded up a truck with a bunch of old furniture from our basement. Dad and I had fought the night before about the divorce papers from Mom. Maybe on another day, I would have just hung out at home. But I wanted to be with him. Maybe I thought I could prove I wanted to live with him."

Already this sounded like a long story. I didn't want Frankie and Andrew to have another run in, but soon, I knew, Andrew would wonder what happened to me.

I tried to hurry the story along. "That's how you found out about the family in the shack. You dropped off the furniture with your dad."

Frankie rubbed her forefinger and thumb together. "I thought he meant to really help them, and it was fun. I felt like I was doing something good. Roxy bounced all around the truck as we brought everything inside and set up the little kitchen." Frankie took a folded piece of paper out of her pocket and passed it to me. "Roxy drew that for me as we finished unloading the truck."

I looked at the crayon-drawn picture of a family cuddled together on a couch, under the words *Our New House* all in capital letters.

"Roxy gave me the picture and said, 'For you, for giving us a house for keeps.'"

Frankie stopped, her eyes watery, the way they'd been last night at the meeting. So strange. Frankie used sarcasm, threats, and insults to get her way, but never before these past two days had I ever seen her show any weakness. Now I'd seen her in tears half a dozen times.

Frankie rubbed her nose before continuing. "Roxy had this look in her eyes, a familiar look, one I probably used to wear back when I thought maybe Mom would come home someday, and we'd be a family again."

"Sadie, you okay?" Andrew called, coming around the corner from the hall into the living room. He stopped when he saw Frankie. "What's going on?"

"Your mom dropped off Frankie." I looked at Frankie, not knowing what else to say.

Frankie shrugged. "I asked her if she knew where Sadie was, and she brought me over. She asked if you'd go chat with her for a second before she leaves, though."

Andrew looked at us for another moment before nodding. "Okay. Just ..." He looked more worried than angry, with creases rippling across his forehead. "Let me know if you need me, Sadie."

My bandages felt thick against my hands, and suddenly, I saw the whole situation from Andrew's point of view. No wonder he was treating me like a fragile vase. I seemed ready to fall to pieces at any minute. This realization, more than anything else, crystallized the pain in me into forward motion, kept me from tumbling down into myself. I didn't want to be a girl who fell apart, a girl at whom people cast worried glances.

"I'm fine," I said, pulling myself back together, wondering if the pieces that used to be me even had the possibility of fitting back together again.

Andrew shoved his feet into his boots and pulled on his coat before going outside. I turned back to Frankie.

The tears were gone, and now she wore a determined expression. "As we left, I heard Dad remind Quinn Thompson about their agreement. That's when I knew the house wasn't for keeps, at least not without strings attached."

"But your dad didn't own that land. You had to know ..."

"He'd been planning to buy it for a while, ever since he heard—" Frankie stopped abruptly. "Well, you know. That Patch might be out there."

Patch's name, coming from Frankie, cut through me,

and I wanted to jump off the couch and grab her by the shoulders and shake her. Just the tiniest bit of information, the one thing Frankie's dad didn't know for sure. He knew a bear was out there, that it was probably Patch, but then when I'd told Frankie without meaning to that we'd hiked out to see Patch, I'd given away the one answer Jim Paulson needed in order to attack Patch one way or the other.

"I shouldn't have told him," Frankie said, so quietly I almost didn't hear her. "Do you know what he said on our drive home from the shack that day? He said, 'People fight for what they want, Frankie. If that man really wants that house, he'll fight for it. People who get handouts end up like your mom, leeching off other people. If you want to help that family so much, fight for it. Help them find the bear.'"

"That's why you pretended to be my friend," I said, working hard to keep my voice even. "To prove to your dad you knew how to fight for something?"

"At first, yes," Frankie admitted. "But then, things just changed."

"You said you wanted help." I couldn't keep the sharp edges out of my voice. As long as she didn't pretend we were friends, I could handle this conversation. But if she acted like she'd wanted to be my friend, she would only confuse me. I couldn't stand any more confusion.

"Dad was outside when the escrow company called, so I took the message. He's supposed to go sign papers at the library, but I didn't tell him. I walked over to your house, to see if you'd go to the library with me to talk to the owner."

"Why ...?" The last place in the world I wanted to be was wherever those papers would be signed. It would be like watching someone sign an order to kill Patch. I couldn't handle it.

"Maybe we can convince him not to sell Dad the land." The words tumbled out of Frankie's mouth now, and she leaned forward, her eyes flashing with intensity. "Then, Dad can't do anything to Patch, and maybe Roxy's family won't have to leave the shack."

I stared at her. "You think ..."

"Maybe it won't work, Sadie, but can't we at least try?"

The landowner had been trying to sell that land for years, and of course, now that he had a buyer, he'd want to sell it no matter what.

But still, I found myself nodding, setting Higgins on the floor and standing up. "We had better hurry, if we want to do this."

Frankie jumped up, ran over, and threw her arms around me in a giant hug. I stood, my arms stiff at my sides, not sure what to do. Frankie didn't hug people.

She stepped back and burst into laughter. "Breathe, Sadie. You ready?"

We put on our winter gear and ran out to Helen's car. "So you girls need a ride to the library?" Helen asked.

"Yes," I said, avoiding Andrew's eyes. I didn't want to explain this all now. "Sorry that you've been a chauffeur all day."

"Sadie, what about the ornaments?" Andrew asked.

I buckled up as I answered. "Do you mind watching them, until I get back? I think this will only take a few minutes."

I looked up in time to see Andrew nod. "You're sure you're all right, Sadie?"

"Yes," I said, finally looking him full in the face. "I promise."

Chapter 28

Escrow

We ran up the sidewalk to the library as fast as we could go without slipping, but stopped, simultaneously, in front of the doors.

Frankie turned to me. "Do you think this will work?"

I hesitated, almost sure it wouldn't. Without really thinking about it, I closed my eyes and breathed a prayer. *Please, God. Not for me, but for Patch and Roxy. Please fix this.*

I opened my eyes. God hadn't made this mess. I had. What right did I have to ask him to fix things now? Still, as my insides tipped back and forth, as my thoughts stalled on the knowledge that I didn't deserve help, a new thought slipped into my mind, as though brushed in under a door.

I am with you.

That was it. Not like a voice, or anything, but this thought clashed so strongly against my own thoughts, I knew it hadn't come from me. I blinked as the storm settled in my mind, as my heartbeat slowed, as I caught my breath. Maybe the landowner would sell the land to Jim. But right now, I felt completely sure of the right thing to do. It had been ages since I felt sure about anything. Maybe someday all the broken edges inside me would find a way to heal.

I smiled at Frankie. "Let's do this."

As soon as we stepped inside, we saw two suited men waiting in the study room. Frankie led the way over to the room, and we went inside.

"Girls, we've reserved this room for a meeting," the man carrying the briefcase said.

"That's what we're here for." Frankie sat at the table. "I'm Frankie Paulson, and this is my friend, Sadie Douglas."

"You took my message," the other man said. "Where's your dad? We've been waiting for over twenty minutes."

"He's not coming." Frankie motioned for me to sit down.

The men folded their arms and gave us matching we-aren't-here-to-play-around looks.

Frankie leaned forward, her elbows on the table, both eyebrows raised. "You own a lot of land around here, right?"

We had talked over the plan on the drive from Vivian's, with a little help from Helen. She said our strongest defense would be to convince the landowner that the DNR would be unhappy if the sale went through. Since this was the truth, convincing him shouldn't be difficult. But whether the DNR's unhappiness would cause him to turn down a sale was a different question.

"Right." The first man, who must be the lawyer, set down his briefcase. "That's why my client is anxious to speak with your dad and sign papers. Is he on his way?"

"We told you our names." Frankie leaned back in her seat and crossed her arms too, not rattled in the least by these guys.

Good thing she'd offered to do most the talking. I'd be tongue-tied and stuttering by now.

The lawyer, or whoever he was, sighed. "I'm Mr. Wallace, and this is my client, Mr. Pearson. And your dad …"

"Plans to force the DNR to remove a hibernating bear from her den after he purchases this land. A bear he thinks is dangerous."

"But she isn't dangerous," I added.

Frankie didn't acknowledge this either way. "As it stands, the bear has three yearlings, all of whom will have to be removed from the den. As you can imagine, the DNR isn't happy about the expense. I don't imagine the DNR will be happy with you, either, if you sell the land."

"Why didn't anyone tell me this?" Mr. Pearson frowned at Frankie. "I can't afford to have the DNR angry with me, not with all the negotiating I do with them over land use."

Mr. Wallace shrugged. "So they're mad. And you've unloaded a piece of land you haven't been able to sell for years."

Mr. Pearson rounded on his lawyer. "So you knew about this?"

"I may have heard rumblings, but I figured you—"

192

"You figured wrong!" Mr. Pearson's voice had risen to a shout. "Not only do I disagree with removing a bear from hibernation in general, I'm on shaky ground with the DNR as it is."

I bit my lip to keep from smiling. This was better than I could have hoped for.

"So you aren't going to sell?" Mr. Wallace asked.

Mr. Pearson gestured impatiently towards Frankie. "Not to this man."

Mr. Wallace snatched his briefcase and strode for the door. "What a waste of time." He turned back to look at Mr. Pearson. "I suppose you don't care who is squatting in that old shack out there. You'll probably get sued for allowing a family to live on uninhabitable land. But don't come running to me for help."

Mr. Pearson looked at us. "So I'm not only losing a great deal of money today. On top of that, I'm likely to be sued?"

Frankie jumped in. "No, I'm sure they wouldn't..."

"Girl, I don't care what you're sure or not sure of. This is real life, and I refuse to let my perpetually unsellable land cost me more money."

"But they don't have a home. They lived in a car before. You can't ..."

"I don't know what you expected, coming here to talk to me," Mr. Pearson said. "I'm not a charity worker. That family needs to get out of that house. I'll go tell them myself."

All of this had happened so fast, the unraveling of the sale, the decision to throw the Thompson family out of the shack, that I could only watch helplessly. I should say something, fight for the Thompsons to keep their home, but I couldn't figure out what to say.

As Mr. Pearson stood to go and Frankie shot me a look that clearly said, *help!* I stammered, "At least let them stay a few more days. Let them stay for Christmas. Please."

Not the strongest argument, I knew, but I didn't have anything else. Mr. Pearson stopped and grimaced at me, as though I'd asked if he'd also string up kittens by their tails.

"They have until the twenty sixth at noon, then. And you tell them. I have no more time for this nonsense." He hurried after Mr. Wallace, leaving me and Frankie staring at the door.

"Well, at least you got what you wanted." Frankie's voice was sharp and sarcastic.

Anger flared up in me, hot and quick, like a firework igniting. "Frankie, either we're on the same side, or we're not. Maybe we don't agree on everything. But how am I supposed to be your friend if every other minute you turn on me?"

Frankie sighed and dropped her head into her hands. "I just ..."

My anger sizzled out, spent just as quickly as it had come. "I know. We just lost the Thompsons their house. So I suppose ..." An idea started to form in my mind.

"What?" Frankie turned to look at me. "What are you smiling about?"

"Let's go see Penny," I said.

From: Sadie Douglas
To: Pippa Reynolds
Date: Thursday, December 22, 6:13 PM
Subject: Re: Hello???!?

I know, I know, Pips, I shouldn't have gone so long without emailing. But so much happened, and I promise to tell you the whole story someday soon, but for now, here's the good news:

Patch is safe! The sale fell through, and the DNR strongly reminded Jim that if anything happens to Patch, he will be considered responsible. So I think she's going to make it through the winter!

We found a new house for the Thompsons! I thought Penny might know of a house where they could stay for a while, maybe someone's lake house that needed housesitting, because I've seen ads like that on the bulletin board. But it turns out that she had a totally amazing idea for a house for the Thompsons, such a good idea that even Frankie can't stop jumping up and down.

Mom is home from the hospital (long story), and I think she is going to be okay for Christmas. Andrew and Helen came to the house to get clothes for us, since we had to spend the night at the hospital, and when I got home yesterday, the Advent calendar was fixed. Pips! The calendar was from Andrew. He's the only one who could have fixed it. I opened all the drawers I missed, and the map is almost all put together. I only have the one last drawer, the twenty-fourth, to open. There is no drawer twenty-five. Where do you think Andrew is sending me?
I can't wait to hear what you think of your present, Pips!

Chapter 29

We Wish You a Merry Christmas

My eyes snapped open, and I shivered with excitement. Christmas Eve. I checked my clock. Five a.m. Too early to run shouting down the stairs, but not too early to open the final drawer in my advent calendar. Outside my window, stars still lit the dark sky as I tiptoed to my desk. The floorboards, as always, were icy, and the temperature in my room felt like it might be thirty degrees, so I hurried back to bed with the calendar and burrowed in under the covers. Higgins lifted his head to check what in the world I was doing, moving around in the middle of the night, huffed, and dropped his chin back onto his paws.

My skin tingled as I reached for drawer twenty-four, and not just because of the chill in the air. Inside, I found an origami candle made from white and yellow paper. I rolled it in my hands, more than ever not wanting to pull the paper folds apart. Pen marks on the base of the candle caught my attention, and I looked closer. *Meet me at six pm.*

I hugged myself with happiness. Today would be the best day ever. I set the calendar aside and pulled the comforter out from under Higgins, who groaned, stretched, and curled up again on the remaining blankets. Cocooned in the comforter, I went to my desk to inspect the map. I'd connected most of the pieces, and now I played with the rest, moving them back and forth until I had connected all the edges. With the exception of the one missing square, the square I would have found on December fourteenth, the map was complete, but nothing marked where I was supposed to go, just paths and notes such as twenty paces to the north. What if the missing piece was essential? But if so ...

I rushed over to the calendar. Sure enough, an origami flower waited inside the fourteenth drawer. I quickly smoothed it out and stumbled over the bulky comforter on my way back to the desk. A red X marked a spot just off the path that wound away from the cartoon of my house, and from the hand-drawn scale at the top of the map, the X appeared to be about a mile away from my house.

I couldn't sit still. I bounded across my room and dressed in paint clothes, so I'd be ready for our house-decorating mission later this morning. Then I finished wrapping the presents I'd bought yesterday, Frankie's sketchbook, and the pink chef's hat I'd found on the clearance rack at Moose

Tracks, a last minute present for Dad. But Andrew. I hadn't bought him anything. I picked up my own sketchbook and started to draw. I lost all track of time as I drew picture after picture of Andrew as I imagined him, hammering the calendar together out of wood, painting, folding origami, hiding the clue in the telescope, finding the calendar broken on the floor and fixing it. The last picture I drew was Andrew, wearing his signature crooked smile, opening his gift from me. In all, I had a series of eight sketches, each three inches by three inches. I added color and texture, layering over my mistakes or letting them simply add to the fun of each drawing. On my way to church, I'd ask Dad to stop by Moose Tracks, where I'd seen a collage frame that held eight pictures, just this size, with the other art supplies.

As I flipped through my pictures one last time, adding tiny details here and there, I heard Dad banging around in the kitchen. My stomach growled as the smell of maple syrup wafted under my door. French toast was traditional on Christmas Eve. I hurried downstairs to help him.

After we served Mom breakfast in bed and stuffed ourselves full, Dad drove me across town, first to Moose Tracks, where I found the frame, and then over to church. Ruth and Frankie already waited in front of the sanctuary, dancing around to keep warm.

"Do they know yet?" I asked Frankie.

She shook her head. "Last they heard, Dad was buying the land, and they had to get out by the end of the week. They're packing up."

Penny pulled up in her lemon yellow Volkswagon Beetle, honking her horn. She leapt out of the car and hurried over to meet us.

"Ruth's dad and Doug are on their way around town collecting donations." She dangled the keys in front of us. "You ready to get busy?"

I linked arms with Ruth and Frankie, and we ran across the church grounds, laughing as we slid on the snow. We went the opposite direction of the treehouse to a little log cabin on the far side of the sanctuary I'd never paid attention to. Not quite as quirky as the treehouse, the cabin still looked like it belonged in a Christmas card. Snow frosted the roof and old-fashioned windowpanes, and the front porch had a swing just like Vivian's. Penny had already delivered the Christmas tree she'd cut down with her crew yesterday. It waited in a tree holder next to the path leading up to the house. Someone had also delivered a stack of buckets, rags, brooms, and mops.

Penny turned the keys in the lock. "Our last caretaker moved out about a year ago. His mom was sick, and he wanted to be closer to her in Florida. We've been looking for someone to take his place ever since. Caretakers watch over the grounds, fix up the buildings, make Sunday morning coffee, and in exchange, this house is theirs."

As soon as she opened the door, Frankie, Ruth, and I tumbled inside. The house had one main living room, two bedrooms, a kitchen, and two bathrooms. Everything was made of stone and logs, so we wouldn't have much to paint, but cobwebs and dust covered every surface. Ruth sneezed.

"Well, girls." Penny tossed us rags from her bucket. "We have our work cut out for us."

We each took a room and went to work clearing the dust. Ruth kept sneezing, and Frankie, as it turned out, was deathly afraid of spiders. She shrieked every time one scurried out of a dark corner. I didn't like spiders much myself, and had to call Penny to save me when I found a nest of them in the bedroom closet. My white bandages turned mud-grey, and I finally took them off, tracing the lines of stitches with my index finger.

Just as we finished wringing out our rags in the sink, when we were ready to flop onto Penny's freshly mopped floor, a horn honked outside.

Doug ran in, followed by Ben and half the rest of the youth group who had caravanned over behind the truck.

Doug nodded in approval. "Looking good, ladies."

The crew brought in rugs, couches, beds, two dressers, bookshelves, dishes, clothing, blankets, a table and chairs, a crib, and boxes of food and supplies. After Penny rebandaged my hands with supplies from her first-aid kit, we rushed from room to room, finding places for everything. We hung clothes in the closets, stacked towels still warm from the dryer in the linen closet, and arranged warm coats on the coat rack by the door. Ben chopped wood outside, filling the wood bin, and brought a stack inside to lay a fire in the grate.

Once we'd put everything into place, we hauled the tree inside. After Penny strung lights on the branches, Claudia and Jasper stacked presents around the tree while Frankie, Ruth, and I hung the ornaments Andrew and I had made. Cameron had donated an iPod and a portable speaker, so he set up a Christmas playlist. Vivian showed up with a collection of her framed artwork, which we hung on the walls. Then she helped us cut fresh pine garland for the mantle, and we wove another strand into a wreath for the door.

Doug put apple cider in a pot on the stove, adding cinnamon sticks and clove, so the air smelled like Christmas. Dad arrived, totally embarrassing me in his *Sugar and Spice and Everything Nice* apron, but still, he brought everything for a Christmas feast, turkey, mashed potatoes, salad, rolls, even gravy.

"Which we'll do right this time," he said, as he set two praline-crusted pumpkin pies into the refrigerator.

Dad organized a cooking team in the kitchen, timing everything so the food would be ready just before three when Andrew and Helen were supposed to deliver the Thompsons to the cabin. At two forty five, we all piled into the back bedroom and waited. Minutes ticked by. We waited, listening to the Christmas music playing in the other room. Finally, we heard voices and footsteps outside. Cameron struck a chord on his guitar, and Doug threw open the door as we started to sing:

We wish you a Merry Christmas
We wish you a Merry Christmas
We wish you a Merry Christmas
And a Happy New Year.

Tears glistened in Roxy's mom's eyes as she held the baby to her shoulder.

"Perhaps I should have warned you," Ruth's dad said, patting Quinn Thompson on the shoulder, "But we're hoping you'll accept a job as a caretaker for the church, along with this house."

Quinn opened and closed his mouth, but couldn't seem to find any words. Finally he choked out, "Thank you, sir. I'd be ... honored. I don't know quite what to say."

Roxy barreled down the hall and threw her arms around me and then around Ruth, and finally around Frankie. "Thank you, thank you, thank you!"

We gave them a tour of their new house and then ushered them to the table, where we served them dinner. Then we waved goodbye, leaving them to celebrate in their new house.

"Thank you, Sadie." Frankie held out a small, wrapped gift. "Open it tomorrow, okay?"

I took her gift out of my backpack and handed it to her. "You too."

I hugged both Frankie and Ruth goodbye, knowing I would see Ruth in a few hours at the cabin for Christmas Eve fondue. But first, it was time for me to go home, wrap Andrew's present, and head out into the woods. I looked for him as I climbed into the Jeep with Dad, but he and Helen were already gone.

"What are you grinning about, Sades?" Dad asked.

Since he already knew the answer to this question, I just grinned some more. Dad blasted Christmas music all the way home.

Chapter 30

Candlelight

I rolled up the taped-together map and put it in my jacket pocket along with the compass. I slid the wrapped frame in my backpack and checked my watch. Five thirty. Time to go.

"Take these." Dad handed me his industrial strength flashlight and his cell phone. "Call if you need anything."

Outside, the sunset had deepened into twilight. I closed the door behind me and crunched out into the quiet snow, wondering what I would say to Andrew. After a few failed attempts in my mind, I gave up. I'd say whatever bubbled out, the way shaken-up soda bursts from its can. For now, I let the quiet of the forest surround me, step after step. Once I had stepped into the trees, I took out the map and compass and began following the instructions. The path through the snow wasn't entirely clear, but Andrew had counted steps and noted them on the map. Forty steps to the northwest. Turn left. Ten steps to the north. Turn right. Fifty steps due west.

As the darkness deepened, I took out my flashlight, only checking the map for each new direction, holding only the light and the compass. My attention tightened to this moment, this next instruction. I knew, somewhere out there, not too far away, Andrew had arranged some surprise for me. If only figuring out life was this easy, with a map, and a compass, and a flashlight to light my way. Maybe then I wouldn't get things so wrong so much of the time.

Images of the last few days, of Frankie and me talking to Mr. Pearson, of the youth group joyfully setting up the cabin, of Roxy's family seeing their new house, floated into my mind.

I stopped walking. For the past few weeks, I'd felt totally lost, as though God was so far away, so impossible to understand. Now, in the past few days, I felt something new happening. As though he was just beyond my reach, beckoning me, replacing my frustration with new thoughts, with a whispered, *Look here. See this?*

Is that you? I whispered into the darkness.

The answer was like silk slipping around my shoulders, softly wrapping around me until it pooled on the ground, so tangible I shone my light on the snow to see if actual fabric laid at my feet. My flashlight's golden light reflected on the white snow, as the answer settled deep into me.

I'm right here.

I looked up, the falling snow streaking white against the black sky, and I breathed in deeply. My arms raised at my sides, and I started spinning, slowly at first, letting the snow kiss my cheeks, and then I spun faster, faster, and faster until I closed my eyes against the dizziness and collapsed in the snow, laughing. I had thought that Andrew's gift was the best present I could imagine, but this was so much better, and I couldn't even put it into words.

Finally, when my head stopped spinning, I opened my eyes and took out my map. Only two directions left. Twenty steps to the northwest and one hundred steps to the north. I hurried on, and when I turned from the northwest to the north, I saw flickering in the trees. I stumbled forward, not worrying about the map anymore. Soon I saw the entire clearing lit by candles stuck directly into the snow. In the center of the clearing, Andrew sat on a red and white plaid picnic blanket, facing away from me. A picnic basket sat beside him.

He started ringing jingle bells.

"So, you've been waiting out here since December first?" I asked.

"Sorry I couldn't have you over to my house the day after Thanksgiving." He stood and turned to look at me. "I was a little busy."

I ran over to him and threw my arms around him, giving him a huge hug, and then stepped back, embarrassed. "I'm sorry I broke the calendar. It wasn't on purpose ... at first. And then I guess I kind of threw a temper tantrum. Thank you for fixing it. And for making it. It's utterly amazing!"

We sat down on the blanket, and he poured hot cocoa for us and took out a selection of Christmas cookies. I took off my gloves, gently pulled his gift out of my backpack and handed it over.

"Was I that obvious?" he asked.

"I didn't know until the calendar was fixed after the hospital," I said.

He grinned. "Good."

He opened his present. He took his gloves off and ran his finger over each scene. Finally he said, "Thank you, Sadie."

His long lashes were shadowy in the candlelight. He held my gaze, his eyes warm and all lit up from the inside. It was the same look he'd given me so many times these past few weeks, the look that had so confused me, but now, finally, it made sense. I felt the same way too, like my happiness had grown too big to fit inside my body and would overflow any minute. He reached over and twined his fingers through mine. I leaned my head on his shoulder, and he put his arm around me.

We sat there in the candlelight for a long time, talking and laughing until the hot cocoa and cookies were gone. I remembered how afraid I had been on Thanksgiving of what would happen if Andrew and I were anything more than friends. *Maybe, Pips*, I said silently. *Maybe he's just the tiniest bit of a crush.*

"Time for Christmas." Andrew stood and helped me up. We blew out the candles and collected them in the picnic basket and his backpack, and I followed him back toward my house.

When Dad threw open the front door, he grinned. "Told you it wasn't me."

Andrew waited with us while Mom finished dressing in the new pajamas Dad bought her for Christmas, and then Dad carried Mom, slippers and all, out to the Jeep. I grabbed my presents for Ruth and Helen, and Andrew scooped up Higgins. We piled into the car and laughed as Dad spun the tires on purpose on the way out the driveway.

Mom told her gravy-disaster stories on the way to the research station, and we laughed so hard we were in tears by the time we arrived. I couldn't tell if I was laughing or really crying, but I knew whatever this feeling was, it had everything to do with happiness. Even though Mom's cheeks were still pale, she smiled her real smile, the smile that crinkled the skin around her eyes.

Dad pulled into the research station. Ruth's family was already there, and we threw open our doors to head inside. I carried Higgins, and Dad carried Mom again. I waited at the front door, holding it for them, feeling the warm air from inside, the smells of spices and Christmas Eve fondue wafting out toward us.

Dad set Mom down inside the door, and suddenly I realized everyone was looking at me.

"What?"

No one answered, but Higgins barked and rushed inside.

I followed him in. "What is it, Higgy?"

I heard a laugh that could only come from one person. "Stop. Down. Not my face," she said.

"Pips?" I shouted, running around the corner.

"Sades!" She threw herself into my arms, and then we were laughing and hugging and she was telling me how hard it was to keep the secret about coming for Christmas.

I dragged her over to introduce her to Ruth, but of course they had already met, and then I hugged Pippa's parents and even her sister, Andrea.

"You better appreciate this, Sades." Andrea tugged on my braids, grinning. "I gave up a big Christmas party for you."

"So, what do you think?" Pippa flopped down on the couch next to me, as everyone settled into the station. "Is it better than a kitten?"

Higgins jumped up on my lap, and Andrew and Ruth piled onto the couch to join us.

"What do you think, Hig? Pips or a kitten? Which do you prefer?"

He barked and licked Pippa's face from chin to hairline, making her shriek and hide her face behind my shoulder. "Make him stop!"

I laughed and laid my head back against the couch, squished between Higgy, Pips, Andrew, and Ruth and let my happiness whirl around me, like the snow in the forest.

"It's perfect, Pips," I said. "Absolutely perfect."

THE END